Texan Secrets

Sheriff Owen Rowlands's closest friend Renard has gone missing. Searching his friend's ransacked house, the lawman finds a dying man on the bed – but no sign of Renard. Determined to track down his friend, Rowlands investigates links to a mysterious gang, only to find that his old friend was not what he seemed.

As he hunts down the gang to their mountain lair, a deadly secret is unravelled, and the sheriff finds that his world is flipped upside down.

Texan Secrets

Dirk Hawkman

A Black Horse Western

ROBERT HALE

© Dirk Hawkman 2018
First published in Great Britain 2018

ISBN 978-0-7198-2633-7

The Crowood Press
The Stable Block
Crowood Lane
Ramsbury
Marlborough
Wiltshire SN8 2HR

www.bhwesterns.com

Robert Hale is an imprint
of The Crowood Press

Typeset by
Derek Doyle & Associates, Shaw Heath
Printed and bound in Great Britain by
CPI Group (UK) Ltd, Croydon, CR0 4YY

For Caroline

PROLOGUE

The menacing blackness of the night had fallen. Not a cricket chirped, nor an owl sang. The ghostly silence only added to Louanne's oppressive sense of dread.

She paced restlessly outside her cabin. The rock of anger and fear in her belly was unbearable. Her lantern did nothing to ward off the suffocating darkness. While she knew that her vigil was pointless, she had to do something. Something!

She knew that her boys were bad. Aged eleven and twelve, they had grown to be physically strong enough to resist her. Chiding and spanking had long ago become impotent punishments against them. They had been thrown out of the schoolhouse. While she toiled and kept the house, they idled their days away. Her boys were already drinking and smoking, and – worst of all – stealing.

Tonight was frighteningly worse, though.

It was not unusual for them to disappear for hours or even days at a time. They had wandered off around noon that day. Louanne had risen early. With no husband, every single task on the land and in the home fell to her.

She had once boasted a cascade of beautiful, ebony hair and piercing blue eyes. That fine hair was now swimming with silver serpents. Over a decade of solitary labour in the fields, and two boys to raise alone, had drained her energy. Her love as a mother had never faded, though she felt like a beast under the yoke, trudging through her drab life one small pace at a time.

Louanne had woken her sons that morning, and warmed some coffee and porridge. They had cussed her with language that would have shocked an outsider. Louanne, though, was well-accustomed to their filthy tongues. The rising sun, the stifling heat, and the seducing scent of breakfast had stirred them, though. The three had chatted contentedly at the table in the centre of the cabin. Louanne was reminded of happier times, when her boys were little. She would, as always, attempt to give her boys instructions.

'Now you two come on out to the fields with me, see. There's a whole lot to be done. I need two strong boys today.'

'Yes, Mother!' her youngest had answered in mock obedience.

She was hoping that her boys would come and help her collect the grain, at least for a while. At times, they did put in some mediocre effort before disappearing to Lord knows where.

Indeed, her sons had been surprisingly supportive that morning. They had followed her out to the field, each carrying a wicker basket. Louanne had felt a pang of pride, if only for a moment. An unwed mother in this county, she was a magnet for spiteful lies and gossip. For a short while, Louanne told herself she was a proud family woman. The sun fixed its unforgiving gaze directly on the fields, yet the three were relieved by a welcome cool breeze.

Louanne and her sons ground away throughout the morning. Their help, and uncharacteristic good behaviour, delighted her. As midday approached, Louanne sent the boys back to the cabin to fix themselves some lunch. She did not expect them to return in the afternoon – and they did not.

Nevertheless, Louanne smiled to herself throughout the afternoon. Lacking a father, it seemed natural that her sons had grown to become unruly and troublesome. Dwelling on her worries for the boys, and her physical fatigue from her labour, eventually tired Louanne's merry spirits. As the sun began to retire, and the air cooled, Louanne paced wearily back to the cabin. Bearing the weight of the basket full of grain, she felt particularly melancholy. Her soul felt as grey as the swelling shadows.

Her shock as she re-entered the cabin was an ugly reveille from her dolour. Her gun cabinet was open and her rifle was gone.

Louanne immediately checked her pockets. Flustered to the point that her vision was misted, her coarse hands somehow found the cabinet key. Louanne had always been mindful of keeping the rifle locked away from her boys. How the heck had they gotten in? The wooden case had not been broken. Had they somehow picked the lock?

Louanne was so fearful that she was unsteady on her feet. She had not touched a drop of liquor for many a year, yet she felt intoxicated as she clumsily forced herself to sit. Her panicked breathing made clear thought a battle.

Over the last couple of years, the schoolteacher, the minister and even the sheriff had brought her boys back. While a mother with no husband was disgraceful enough, it was the inkling of pity which she detected in the townsfolk that she found the most shameful. Louanne had fed and taught the boys, loved them, even beaten them when needed, but they were young varmints in the making. She had never surrendered her hope of making them good honest men. But now? What now?

Fooling around with guns was a stride beyond. What if they hurt somebody? What if – and Louanne sprang to her feet at this possibility – they hurt themselves?

She did not know where they had disappeared to. While they were only eleven and twelve, they were too old, and too defiant, for Louanne to run around after them. Exhausted, hungry, and shackled by worry, Louanne did not know what her next act should be.

The following hours were a marathon of terror. She paced her cabin in nightmarish circles.

Louanne wondered whether she should ride in to town, stay put, head over to the next farm, or simply pray. Neither the moon, nor a single star, pricked the suffocating black blanket of the sky. Only her lantern, whose light was already dying, created a tepid ring of radiance. As the lamp finally failed, Louanne pressed her back against the wooden wall of the cabin and wept. Never had she known such despair nor horror. She slid down the wall and embraced her knees. Her hopeless sobs were the only sound that rang through the eerie gloom.

Louanne did not know how long she had lain slumped in the darkness, but she was roused from her petrified trance by the sound of laughter. She rose, and lit the lamp again. As it cast its eye into the night, Louanne glimpsed shadowy movement.

'Mother! Mother! Mother!' her boys chirped joyfully.

Taken aback by their high spirits, Louanne could not resist trapping them against her chest. She held them both for some time, as her two sons continued to chat excitedly. Louanne could feel the rifle strapped to her eldest boy's back. Her fingertips also found wet, warm spots on his shirt. The coppery smell was unmistakeable. Blood.

'Where the heck have you boys been?! I've been worried to death about you.'

Despite the shadows, Louanne could make out her first-born's macabre smile.

'Guess what, Mother? Daddy came to visit us!'

CHAPTER 1

Owen Rowlands commanded great respect from the schoolchildren he taught. However, it was not only fear of Owen's ugly wrath that inspired good behaviour from Prospect's boys and girls. He was also the town's sheriff.

True, he won the position pretty much because nobody else wanted it. Prospect was a frontier town with barely a hundred settlers. The meagre sheriff's pay was hardly worth the nuisance of accosting drunks, breaking up fights and tracking down missing cattle.

Nevertheless, Owen's pupils were enthralled by his (sometimes embellished) accounts of his adventures.

He was physically unnerving, with the shoulders of a bull and a similar manner. Some said that he was ill-suited to his profession. The challenge of educating the youngsters of Prospect had tested him. He was still a young man, yet grey spots were already sprouting in his sandy hair and meticulously neat beard. While he was, at his core, kind and decent, he had to constantly fight to prevent his anger from exploding. Indeed, he often found the challenges of a lawman much easier than that of an educator.

Owen had been suggested for the post of school-teacher by his predecessor, Phillipe Renard. Owen had been a favourite pupil of Renard. Struck by Owen's great intelligence, when Owen had reached manhood, he and Renard had become close friends. Renard – so it was said – came from money, and had been educated in a college on the East Coast. There was something of the eccentric professor about Renard. Clever and funny, he too had been much loved by his students. When he retired, to a very comfortable house outside of town, Renard and Owen had continued their friendship.

It was Saturday afternoon. The untiring attentions of the boiling sun added to Owen's exhaustion from his week at the blackboard. Having slept a little later than usual, Owen was setting out on foot to visit Renard. The retired teacher lived two miles away in his fine brick house. Renard had arranged its construction when Owen was only a boy. The building was furnished expensively with art and décor from all over the world. Renard did indeed enjoy the finer things.

Owen and Renard often met to share a meal and a glass of whiskey. The young sheriff had a beautiful sweetheart who taught at the Sunday School. Renard, though, was a determined lifelong bachelor. Owen had never known him to court, yet Renard sometimes hinted at fiery romances from his youth. With his snowy locks and easy charm, Owen supposed that this winter fox had had its vixens.

The subject of romance had come up a couple of times. On these occasions, Renard had deftly changed the subject. The lawman had never pressed Renard. Many, many settlers in the West were boldly leaving

13

unhappy lives to start again. It was never known why Renard walked away from a well-to-do background to teach in Texas. Prospect was appreciative of his abilities, though.

The heat felt heavy on Owen as he pushed on through the rusty orange soil towards Renard's house. He could see it in the distance, through the blur of the heat. The thick earth seemed to slow his stride. Normally, Owen looked forward to his visits to Renard. Today, though, his sheriff's antennae were vibrating. His time as a lawman had developed in Owen an intuition for trouble. He could break up fights before they started. Owen had at one time suggested an alternative route to a cattle train – and later learned that, almost mystically, he had diverted them from a Red Indian raid.

Though the sky was a serene ocean blue, Owen could feel something in his bones, a danger that was just below the horizon.

That danger manifested its first physical sign when Owen reached Renard's door, which was wide open. This omen energized Owen, and he seized his Colt before stealthily creeping inwards.

Renard's downstairs lounge had been wrecked. There were shattered vases on the fine red carpet, and the leather armchair was upturned. Owen felt like there was an electric current running though him. He forced his professional instincts to dominate the concern for his friend that was burning him like acid. Wiping a bullet of sweat from his brow, Owen swiftly surveyed the other downstairs room. There was nothing out of place there – nor was there any sign of Renard.

Owen climbed the stairs with measured, careful steps.

Though it only took a few seconds to reach upstairs, his ascent felt maddeningly long. It was as if the air was filled with a volatile gas.

Outside Renard's bedroom, Owen noticed that the door was ajar. The sheriff spied through the crack, but could only see the wall beyond. Despite the thick, stifling air, Owen recognized the distinctive copper smell of blood. With a violent kick, Owen struck the door and pointed his weapon into the room as the door swung. It took great restraint for Owen not to pull the trigger when he saw the individual inside.

Lain on Renard's bed was a dying man. The intruder was perhaps eighteen, with ruddy skin and dark hair. The stranger wore a plain white shirt and dirty long johns, but his clothes were torn and bloody. He had obviously been very badly assaulted. The casualty lay on his back, his eyes staring blankly, but Owen could expertly sense slight breathing.

Mindfully, Owen moved towards the intruder. He rested one hand flatly on the stranger's chest, and gripped his revolver tightly with the other. The contact made the man shudder, and groan unintelligibly through broken teeth.

'Partner, I'm here to help you. Can you tell me your name? Can you tell me what happened to you?' Owen hoped that his inner fear was not reflected in his outwardly calming words.

Agonizingly, the stranger turned his head to try and answer, but failed.

He was dead.

CHAPTER 2

Shocked by his gruesome discovery, Owen had to force himself to start thinking like a lawman. The stink of blood and sweat, along with his own fear, made him feel nauseous. Fighting the sickening compulsion to vomit, Owen sprinted to open the window. The thirsty air was little relief, and he wiped his soaking face with his hand. Leaning outside, Owen took greedy breaths.

He rested there for several minutes, until he felt steadier. Owen could see the gentle bustle of Prospect a couple of miles away. The town he protected had its instances of shootings and fights from time to time. His friend's disappearance, and this odd murder, were striking in their gravity and strangeness, though. The baking sun seemed to observe the land below like the watchful eye of a demonic cyclops.

Owen's thoughts were confused. He was at once affronted by the evil crime that had been perpetrated, and saddened that his friend had vanished.

Owen returned his Colt to its holster. He absent-mindedly put his hands in his pockets, where he felt the hard metal of his sheriff's badge. Owen was only a part time law enforcer, and did not always wear the symbol on his breast. He took the badge out of his pocket, and playfully turned it over and over in his hand. Normally, he was very proud to wear the iron star, but that was when he had to do little more than drag unresisting drunks to the jailhouse. Owen reflected how pathetic the little badge now looked. He felt as if it had only been part of a costume in a pantomime. This tiny piece of metal was meaningless. Yet, Owen felt the colossal weight of his duty like a haystack on his shoulders.

Reluctantly, Owen pinned the badge to his waistcoat. The wave of nausea had passed – for now. Owen could feel a clammy layer of sweat between his skin and clothing. Feeling slightly calmer, Owen decided to make a search of Renard's property. The dead stranger could no longer be helped.

With his blackened eyes and misshapen nose, the intruder was most certainly no friend of Renard.

Owen returned to the downstairs lounge. Renard loathed dusting and cleaning, and paid a lady from Prospect to look after his housekeeping. Normally plush and welcoming, the living room had been ransacked. Owen noted, though, that Renard's paintings were untouched. No connoisseur himself, Owen had been assured by Renard that they were valuable. Something occurred to Owen. He entered the dining room which – itself – had not been despoiled. Owen lifted the lid of the wooden case on a table against the wall. He discovered that Renard's silver cutlery had not been stolen.

There had been an invasion of Renard's home, but it had not been a robbery. The disarray was either pure vandalism – or the signs of violent struggle. A man of

17

mature years, Renard was gentle and retiring. Owen could not visualize Renard fending off his aggressors. Had he been kidnapped? While it was an open secret that Renard had more than a little money in the bank, Owen did not know of any living family of Renard.

While Owen and the retired schoolteacher had been close friends for many years, it suddenly struck Owen that Renard's background was a little mysterious. He could not have paid for his townhouse with his paltry teacher's wages. Owen knew that Renard belonged to a wealthy East coast family – so why relocate to a Western frontier town? Renard had always been charming, generous and dedicated to Prospect. He had been an excellent schoolmaster and a regular face at the church on Sundays. While unusual in his wealth, Renard had often received visitors in his home.

Indeed, Renard had been such a force for good in the town, that the folk – himself included – had chosen not to ask too many questions. Well, that was going to change. Owen would need to investigate his old friend thoroughly.

Returning to the wrecked living room, Owen began picking up leaves of paper from the ground. Renard's bureau had been smashed, and his paperwork scattered. Owen organized the sheets into a single pile, and went through the items individually.

Much of it was unsurprising. Correspondence from the bank, letters from a pension company in Boston, ownership documents relating to the house – but only a single personal letter. It was dated just over a year ago, and written in a thick, angry script that was difficult to decipher. The letter was an unexpected glimpse into

Renard's history. Owen felt a flicker of shame that he was intruding into his friend's private business, but read on.

My darling nephew Phillipe,

Well . . . how long has it been? No letters, no Christmas cards, no visits, no nothing! Dont you ever think about your sweet old Aunt Jasmine? Was down in the saloon the other night and got chatting to a handsome young man from Prospect (yes, even at my age, men still fawn over me). Over a glass of whiskey (or two!) he told me a couple things about him and about Prospect and your name came up! Can you imagine my surprise? My little nephew a schoolteacher – hows about that? Well you always were a smart one!

Why dont you write to me? Come to see me? Or maybe I'll come and visit you! Would you like that? Could tell the honest folk of Prospect a thing or two about their dear old schoolmaster!

Thinking of you. . . .

. . .

Aunt Jasmine

Owen was adept at seeing the signs of an individual's inner character. As a schoolmaster, he had reviewed countless essays and tests, and could detect personality traits from a person's handwriting. It was not difficult to see, though, that this Jasmine was bitter and spiteful. The yellowed paper had spots of what could only be whiskey. Never had Renard mentioned an Aunt Jasmine. Her letter, though, suggested that she may not have been the pride of the family.

The letter was dated nearly a year ago from an address

in Brecon county. Owen realized that as part of his inquiries, he may have to pay this Aunt Jasmine a visit himself. The threatening tone of the letter was not well-hidden. As caring and decent as Renard was, he clearly had an enemy.

CHAPTER 3

Reflecting that there was so much that he did not know about Renard, Owen continued his search.

He did not know what he was looking for. The sheriff decided to try an examination of the corpse. Returning upstairs, he felt no shame in rummaging through the pockets of the dead man. The pockets of the stranger's pants only contained a few dollars, and what seemed to be a red handkerchief. It was neatly folded, and Owen unravelled the item. It was a large handkerchief, and crimson red. Owen wondered if the intruder had used the cloth to disguise his face during robberies – if, indeed, the stranger was a thief. A further look at the dead man's damaged face, though, suggested to Owen that the stranger was not eligible for sainthood.

Owen began rifling through the wardrobe and chest of drawers. There was no rulebook in this situation, and the sheriff depended on his instincts and intelligence. Going through Renard's clothes one item after another,

Owen began to realize the immensity of the task before him. He would need to find his old friend, with no apparent witnesses and a hazy idea of Renard's past. Owen would also need to identify the dead man. He did not know how Aunt Jasmine fit into the picture – if at all. Perhaps he could then learn what mysterious encounter occurred in Renard's house.

The sheriff was not surprised at the quality of Renard's clothing. The wardrobe contained a number of expensive suits and shirts. The retired teacher was known for being exceptionally well-attired. Inspecting the wardrobe thoroughly, Owen found nothing of note, until he felt inside the breast of one of Renard's suits. The sheriff's fingertips immediately recognized the cold, hard metal of a Colt revolver.

The weapon was concealed in an inner pocket. Owen withdrew the gun and eyed it attentively. The sight of the gun brought back a memory of Renard that the lawman had not thought on for some time.

Renard had been away for a couple of weeks. From time to time, the retired schoolmaster travelled back East. The sheriff always imagined he had distant relatives to visit, or perhaps business to attend to. Renard was such a private person, and such a dear friend to Owen, that the lawman had never pried. The sheriff had kept an eye on Renard's house during his absence. On the day of his scheduled return, Owen decided to drop by to welcome his old friend back.

The lawman had found the front door wide open. This was not at all unusual for Renard. He was a friendly, hospitable man who would fondly share his time with just about anybody. The sheriff had entered, only to be taken aback by the state in which he found Renard.

He was sat in his armchair, and on his table was a bottle of whiskey. It was half-empty, and there was another, completely empty container on the ground. The whole room stunk like a distillery.

Renard did not notice Owen. Though it was only the early afternoon, and the sun was fixing its fiery vision on Prospect, Renard was dressed in pyjamas and a dressing gown. He was mumbling to himself. In his left hand was a glass of whiskey, in his right – to the lawman's alarm – was a Colt revolver. As Renard muttered drunken non-senses, he playfully cocked the weapon and pulled the trigger repeatedly. The gun was mercifully unloaded, but this did not ease the lawman's discomfort. The old man also waved his whiskey glass as if in time to music that only he could hear.

'Renard!' Owen called. 'Renard, are you OK? Have you been drinking?'

The retired schoolmaster did not answer. It was as if he was totally unaware of the sheriff's presence.

To Owen, the scene was unsettling in a number of ways. The lawman had often enjoyed a drink with Renard, but in his many years, the sheriff had never seen Renard intoxicated. It was saddening to see his friend in such a condition, and Owen pondered what had pro-voked Renard to act thus. It was not odd for Renard to have to travel back East on occasion. Had he encoun-tered something on his journey that had upset him, the lawman wondered.

Nor had the sheriff ever seen Renard handle a weapon. Owen had no idea that Renard even owned a Colt. His friend had never, ever referred to it.

The lawman tiptoed up to the armchair. Renard continued to be lost in his unintelligible drunken soliloquy. Owen gently laid a palm on Renard's shoulder.

'Partner, let me help you to your bedroom.'

The lawman was about to hook his hand under Renard's shoulder, when Renard abruptly rose to his feet and turned his head directly to face the sheriff. So unexpected was the movement that Owen recoiled in fright. It was as if another man was wearing Renard's skin.

'How many children did Zeus have, Rowlands?' Renard's voice was rasping and cruel. Tiny flickers of spit landed on the lawman's face. This would ordinarily have provoked a great rage in the sheriff. In the strangeness of the situation, though, Owen did not react.

'Answer me, boy!'

The lawman played along. The sheriff happened to know the answer, for Renard often spoke of Greek myths.

'Ninety-two, sir.'

Renard's eyes bulged in delight, and he smiled maniacally. What's gotten in to you, Renard, Owen asked himself. You are most certainly not yourself today.

The old schoolteacher patted the lawman on the shoulder.

'Well done, Rowlands. Ninety-two. You would have made a good son to me. Smart. Brave. Not like—'

Renard cut himself off. He closed his eyes, wincing as if he had said something he should not have. It made the lawman curious. Not like what, or who? Had Renard ever married or had children? The old man was so guarded about his history and family that the sheriff had never pressed him.

Renard had rambled on about Zeus and his children.

Though at first alarmed, Owen began to feel embarrassed. Not for himself, but for his former schoolteacher. It was very out of character for Renard to behave in this way. Frustrating and exasperating as it was, the lawman talked Renard into handing over the mysterious Colt and retiring to bed.

Renard had been highly apologetic the next day. Owen had brushed the encounter off, putting it down to the fatigue of a long journey. Heck, it was not as if the lawman himself had never, ever overdone it.

The sheriff had not thought on the encounter for several years. The reappearance of the Colt had awoken this dormant memory, though.

The sheriff returned Renard's Colt to the inner pocket of the suit.

He next turned his attention to Renard's chest of drawers. Under different circumstances, Owen would have felt like a clown comically going through Renard's undergarments and socks. Now, though, the sheriff was intrigued. In just one day, a number of little secrets was making Owen question his perception of his old friend. Kneeling down, Owen opened each drawer and checked its contents thoroughly. He wondered what his inspections of the drawers would reveal and he grinned for a moment as he reflected that he was unlikely to find any further riddles amongst Renard's underwear.

True enough, Renard's chest of drawers did not reveal any perplexing secrets, except one.

In the old teacher's bottom drawer was a crimson red handkerchief, identical to the dead stranger's.

CHAPTER 4

It had felt like an ordeal to return on foot to Prospect under the prickling sun. Owen immediately sent for his two deputies, and they rode back to Renard's house towing a cart. Whoever the stranger was, he deserved better than to be wrapped in blankets and bundled onto the back of a wooden trolley. Owen would see to it that the dead man received a decent burial.

The three were carefully wrapping the corpse. Owen's deputies were good men, and they did not flinch at the ugly task they had. They were the only folk from Prospect who knew of the uncanny event. There were no crowds of curious onlookers, nor ghouls. For now. The sheriff and his men were grateful for that.

'What do you figure happened here, Sheriff?' asked Elijah, one of Owen's faithful deputies. Like Owen, Elijah was a volunteer law officer. He was an earnest, red-headed young man who normally worked at his father's drugstore. Skinny and unimposing, Elijah was a true do-gooder. Owen saw him as a cross between a choir boy and a gunman. Even in the grisly circumstances, the deputy was cheerful and energetic.

Jeremiah, the other deputy, listened carefully. He was a towering man, built like a slab of rock. Owen put his age at around thirty, but Jeremiah's hair was already as silver as flint. Jeremiah did odd jobs around Prospect, but Owen sensed in him a keen intelligence. Jeremiah said little, but deceptively heard and remembered everything. Today, Owen was thankful for Jeremiah's silent attentiveness – and his muscles.

Drained by the afternoon's experience, Elijah's questions were testing Owen's patience. While the sheriff valued Elijah's loyalty and zeal, he was most certainly in no mood for chat.

'I never thought I'd countenance it, but I got a reckoning Renard's been kidnapped,' Owen replied curtly. 'No money, nor anything else stolen. Only the house's been turned upside down.

'And who is this? That's another piece of the puzzle.'

'Gonna be an awful lot t'do, Sheriff. Attend to this dead stranger, search the house—'

'Gonna have to think on all that, Elijah,' Owen cut Elijah off. The sheriff was staying silent in regards to the mysterious items he had uncovered. 'Let's just take this goner to the doc.'

'Yes, Sheriff.' Owen's brusqueness did not put a scratch in Elijah's boyish devotion.

Elijah, Owen, and Jeremiah took the dead man out to the cart. The sheriff locked the door after them, and they rode into town. Owen felt a flicker of guilty dread. There would be no avoiding the intrusive glares and questions of the curious now.

Prospect was a couple of miles away, giving Owen a little time to ride alongside Jeremiah and ask what he thought. Jeremiah was a true confidant to Owen. The deputy's calm had always been a vital complement to Owen's unpredictable anger.

'What do you think, Jeremiah? Gotta admit, this whole situation's a shock t'me. Renard and me been friends a long, long time.'

Jeremiah paused thoughtfully before answering.

'Sheriff – let me tell you a little story. I ain't much older than you and you been the schoolteacher a few years. When I was a schoolboy, Master Renard – as we called him – was the teacher. Now my folks were just farmhands. They wanted me to get some schooling, but oftentimes I had to cut class to go and help them. Not unusual in Prospect, and Master Renard was agreeable to it. Even when I was a boy, I could tell that he cared about us boys and girls. He never gave us no earfuls f'cutting class.'

Jeremiah stopped a moment to wipe his soaking brow. Owen was intrigued by Jeremiah's considered loquaciousness. In the corner of his eye, he noticed Elijah eavesdropping.

'Sure, Renard had to beat us some. But he was a kind, patient man and he only beat you if you was real, real bad. I mean stealing, bullying, lying. Renard never had no sons of his own. So when he said "This is going to hurt me a lot more than it hurts you" before strapping some kid, I think he meant it. A peaceful man.

'So this is something I remember, back from when I was a boy. Me and my brother were playing up in the hills. Just fooling around, walking through them woods, when we heard shots. We ran to see what they were, and who did we see? Master Renard, with a rifle on his shoulder, taking target practice.'

It was odd for Jeremiah to be so talkative, and Owen could sense unease in his deputy.

'He spotted us, and called us over. We was so excited. We loved Master Renard anyway but to see that such an old man was such a good shot – well! He gave me an' my brother a turn with his rifle, and we took shots against the trees for quite some time.

'As you know, Sheriff, Renard is – what's the word? – an *eccentric*. I told all my friends about Renard shooting. You may even remember the day yourself. For a day or two we gossiped. Then we forgot all about it.

'I never thought about that day we found Renard in the woods again, until today. Nothing crazy about a man from Prospect taking rifle practice, Sheriff. Even a dear old teacher like Renard. But we never saw him shooting before. Or after.'

Owen nodded raptly. Jeremiah's encounter reminded the lawman of the incident in which he had found Renard raving drunkenly. The episodes were snippets of the secret side of a deeply private man.

They were drawing into town now. A sneaky gust of wind threw red dust into Owen's eyes. It did nothing to improve his mood. Though blinded for a second, the sheriff noticed a couple of people rubbernecking at the men and their odd delivery.

Jeremiah continued.

'Now you look up *eccentric* in a dictionary. It'll say something like 'set in his ways', or 'this dude's a real character'. You know what I think? Eccentric's just a fancy word for weird.'

Jeremiah had an ingenuous way of putting it. Renard. Weird.

CHAPTER 5

Irritated by the prying eyes and noses of the townsfolk, the three rode directly to the examination room of Crock the Doc. The physician was waiting for them in great excitement.

Doctor Crocker was in fact a cousin of Elijah, and shared his boyish enthusiasm.

No college boy was Crock. Renard had once eruditely described Crock as an autodidact, or barefoot doctor. Apprenticed under the former medical man, the doctor had learned from first hand experience what treatments succeeded, and which failed. Crock was an able man, and adept at extractions, fevers and amputations. Reading the secret stories of the dead, though, was a young science. This was a new skill where the doctor applied his intellect and imagination.

As the deputies positioned the stranger on Crock's table, the medical man could not resist grinning in delight. Crock was fascinated by police work. He adored the tales which Elijah recounted to him, and was thrilled to be playing a part.

'Good afternoon, officers. What can you tell me 'bout

this here cadaver?' Crock was trying his best to come across as serious.

The doctor listened to Owen's account of his visit to Renard's.

'It's over to you, now, Doc. We got to bury this here stranger soon as we can. Anything you can tell us?'

The doctor set to work. He stripped the body, and began his examination.

The doctor looked between the fingers and toes of the dead man. He looked under his tongue, and felt his chest, arms and legs. Crock ran his fingers through the body's hair. Using a nail file, he scraped underneath the stranger's fingernails and toenails.

Owen and his deputies observed in rapt silence. Though they said that dead men tell no tales, Crock seemed to be gleaning valuable information.

'Sheriff, let me show you a couple things. First, this man was beaten to his demise. You don't need a doctor to tell you that. He was beaten with fists or blunt objects. There are no signs of lacerations from a blade, nor wounds from firearms. The body has broken ribs, broken arms and legs, and broken fingers. Now take a look at this.'

The doctor raised the body's arm, revealing the left side of the man's chest. Crock wiped away the blood with a sponge. The flesh was already a kaleidoscope of bruising, but amongst the painful colours, the physician had spotted something.

'Can you see this thick red sore? He's such a mess that it's not easy to make out. This is a burn mark. Very common in these parts. Take a step closer, Sheriff.'

As Owen took a pace nearer, Crock ghoulishly sniffed

the dead man's fingertips. The doctor stifled a giggle as he beckoned Owen to do the same.

'Take a sniff, Sheriff. Do you recognize the smell?'

Owen took a rapid whiff, but did not linger. There was a chemical smell on the dead man's hands. It was a familiar scent, but Owen could not place it.

'It's dynamite, Sheriff. I would hazard a guess that this young man worked with the stuff, possibly in a mine. Oftentimes, I treat dynamite men who have been exposed to explosions, and carry burns such as this. I also noticed sand between his toes – rather than only mud or dust. So I would say that it's likely that this here stranger had been working in the Saint Jude Gold Mine.'

Saint Jude's was perhaps fifty miles away. The mine was not unlike a military camp. The miners sometimes came in to Prospect. They lived in tents out in the desert. The mine was a real magnet for men on the run, and drifters with little to lose. It was perilous work, with dangers from collapsing mines and explosions. Owen wondered how desperate someone had to be to dig for gold for a few pennies and a bowl of broth.

The mystery man was probably not even twenty years old. It seemed as though he had toiled at Saint Jude's, before suffering an agonizing thrashing. Owen rued the waste of a young man's life, but suspected that the stranger was a criminal. He had yet to learn the crook's involvement in Renard's disappearance. Despite Owen's fears, the sheriff felt a touch of pity at seeing the outsider laid out on the table, stripped, and observed by strangers. As a lawman, Owen had to put private feelings aside. No matter what the interloper had done, Owen knew what to do next.

In Prospect, it was customary for the dead to be interred within hours of their passing. Elijah, Jeremiah and Owen proceeded directly to the small cemetery. The three felt drained, yet there was a final task to be undertaken. The sheriff did not want idle tongues gibbering imagined tales. He could not instruct the usual gravediggers in this situation. Owen and his deputies themselves excavated the burial place. The men of Prospect were accustomed to hardship. In fatalistic silence, they dug into the dusty soil. Even Elijah was muted, though he laboured alongside his brother lawmen with grim tenacity.

As the sun slipped into its hiding place behind the hills, the town minister and Doctor Crocker came to join the three. Owen and his men were blackened by dirt which clung to their perspiring flesh. Despite their filthy appearance, they respectfully lowered the coffin into the rocky soil. They bowed their heads as the preacher said a prayer for the nameless corpse.

The party at the graveside resembled a coven of witches. So murky were the law enforcers that, in the sickly moonlight, they all but faded into the shadows. The words of the minister sounded forbidding. He was a man of God, of course. Yet, in the sinister tableau at the graveside, he could easily have been a warlock invoking an ancient rite.

The day was over. Owen did not feel that there was any further police work that he could do that evening. At sunrise, the sheriff would take the next steps in his investigation.

Tonight, though, he had other business on his mind.

CHAPTER 6

After dismissing his deputies, Owen was reluctant to return to his bachelor's room at the boarding house. He longed to be in the arms of his sweetheart Mary, and wearily wrought his way to her homestead.

Only nineteen, Mary lived with her parents in their small house. While she spent much of the week supporting her parents on their farm, Mary Bolton was also Prospect's Sunday School teacher. Her golden locks and slender figure made her strikingly attractive. She had always been embarrassed by the impotent stares of the townsmen, and tried to mask her beauty by wearing a bonnet and a plain dress whenever she could. Her folks were highly watchful of her. It was only with Owen that she felt that she could show her inner passion.

Owen had been calling on her for over a year. While Ma and Pa guarded her closely, they approved of Owen's affections. They would be proud to see her married to Prospect's schoolteacher and sheriff. Indeed, Ma and Pa had impatiently quizzed Owen on the subject several times.

The sheriff rapped on their door. Though it was only

early evening, he knew that Mary's family would be retiring soon. The three would be rising at dawn for their gruelling day on the fields. Owen had rapidly washed his hands and face, but was still filthy from his graveside attentions.

'Sheriff!' Ma answered the door. 'Come on in. What the heck happened to you?' It was comforting to Owen to be received by Mary's ma.

On hearing the visitor at the door, Mary rose from her seat and sprang towards the door. She could not conceal her delight at seeing her suitor. Mary reached out to embrace Owen, but suddenly recoiled – settling for a kiss to Owen's cheek – when seeing Owen's soiled clothes.

'I'll tell you.' The three welcomed Owen in.

He had lost his own folks some time ago. Owen felt at ease with Mary's parents. Though they continued to address him as Sheriff, they also insisted to Owen that he called them Ma and Pa. They were hard workers, and churchgoers. Owen trusted them and explained the day's odd events. They listened raptly. The Boltons were highly private, and most certainly no gossips.

Pa Bolton was intrigued, yet concerned for Owen. He stroked his chalky white beard thoughtfully. Puffing on his pipe, Pa asked Owen how he could support him.

'There is one favour I dare to ask, Pa. It's an imposition and I know it. But I'm gonna be real busy, like. Fixing to ride on out of Prospect first light.'

'Speak, Sheriff.' Pa was still immensely strong, though old enough to have an adult child. He had always been a rigid – yet devoted – father. Pa had never failed to be flexible in regards to Owen's police work.

'I'm asking for Mary to take charge of the schoolhouse for a few days. I intend to wrap this whole business up real quick, like.'

Owen hated to ask, but knew he could depend on the Boltons. Mary had stood in for him many times. The children adored her. Mary had always professed how much she had enjoyed the experience.

Ma and Pa magnanimously agreed. Just before they headed off to bed, Pa winked knowingly at the couple. 'I'll leave you with your gentleman friend for a little while. Don't stay up too late.' Pa smiled kindly.

Though he described Owen's romance playfully, this was a sign of the great confidence they had in him. Ma and Pa would never leave their daughter alone with just anybody.

They could not resist each other anymore. Not even Owen's stink could deter Mary from trapping him in her arms and kissing him passionately. She ached for Owen's touch, her thoughts nearly sinful.

Mary pressed her cheek against Owen's ursine breast. He, too, wondered, when they would be sharing the night under the same roof. As much as Owen aimed to be a model citizen, he had not been raised in a monastery. His passion for Mary was painful – yet he waited. He loved Mary and wanted their life together to be perfect. They had to whisper breathily.

'Honey, Ma and Pa have been asking again.' Mary grinned knowingly. Owen returned their smile.

'You know I love you, my darling. I don't make no big bucks as a schoolmaster. I can't be raising no family in the boarding house.' Owen never whimsically asked himself, 'Oh, what does she see in me?' like some English poet. He could sense Mary's devotion to him, and his promises were not hollow. Owen would wed Mary when he had the means to provide.

'I know, honey.'

Owen truly felt like a piece of dung as he returned to his solitary room. He had a beautiful woman willing to do anything for him. Her own parents also loved him like a son. Owen was genuinely thankful for his good fortune.

Though the Boltons were not wealthy, he wondered what it would be like to share their home and their lives. Their kindness touched him. Just as they would never forsake him, he was resolved to live as the man that Mary deserved.

As he lay down to rest, Owen's mind was a nest of snakes. His body was taut from the day's deadly labours, and refused to unravel. Though he turned over in his bed, the sheriff could find little peace. By the time the dawn's uninvited rays shone through the cracks in the curtain, Owen was not certain whether he had been asleep or not.

While some men are merely cantankerous in the morning, Owen could be as vicious as a cougar. He ripped open the drapes, angrily facing the unwelcome sunlight from his upstairs bedroom. Drawing strength from his rancour, Owen washed and dressed. The sheriff was ready for a battle.

Owen did not see the prone figure watching him from the street below.

CHAPTER 7

Brother Joshua had also had a sleepless night – although Brother Joshua rarely slept, if at all. He was neither a friar nor a priest. Brother Joshua was merely a cruel nickname. He was in fact the town drunk. The people of Prospect tended to be honest and God-fearing, and Joshua very much survived because of their Christian charity. To them, he was only a comedy character, a harmless derelict. They did not know of his inner agony.

He was styled Brother Joshua because sometimes the angels implored him to testify. Joshua would accost passers-by, extolling his visions and warning of what would come to pass. Some ignored him, some humoured him, some cursed him. His untamed beard and hair, and bloody eyes, no doubt caused fear in others.

Lately, his visions had been especially potent. The division between his farsightedness and the real physical world was blurred more than ever. The whispers from the heavens (if that indeed was where they originated) had been relentless. Night after night, he had paced the

dusty streets, speaking out loud and sometimes screaming. Nobody listened. Only rye or whiskey could quell
him for a time. Alcohol did not stymie the visions nor the
voices. If he drank enough of it, though, and he needed
a lot, the resulting incapacitation gave him the pretence
of some rest.

On one occasion, he found himself in the jail cell.
Sheriff Rowlands had taken him there – or so he was
told. Joshua could not remember. The sheriff had asked
Doctor Crocker to look in on him. Joshua had not
resisted the doctor's questions and physical examina-
tions. He was touched by the compassion shown by the
doc and the sheriff. The doctor had said that he thought
that Joshua had some kind of biological ailment. Over
the following months, Crock the Doc had given Joshua
many different medicines. None of them had relieved his
evil eye.

At dawn, he had been lying in an alley, and noticed
the sheriff stirring at his window. Oddly, the sheriff had
been appearing in the seer's waking nightmares. The
lawman's hazy, transparent spirit form had been swimming in a red, ethereal mist. The spirit had been chased
by hideous monstrosities, canine demons with hungry
fangs. At the moment when the wolf-like creatures cap-
tured their prey, Joshua had snapped out of the dream –
until it started again.

Joshua found it difficult to distinguish his irresistible
urges from pure intoxication. He had been sipping on a
stolen whiskey bottle throughout the night. As the sun
rose, Joshua realized that he was still drunk. He felt the
rising, maddening compulsion to confront the sheriff.
Joshua began pacing, swallowing the last slugs of the

booze. The human deep inside him begged Joshua to stop, to refrain. Sheriff Rowlands was a good man. He did not need to deal with a man possessed (as Joshua often thought he was). Joshua did not realize that he was ranting and foaming at the mouth as he walked in circles in the dust, like a rabid hound pursuing its own tail.

No! No! Joshua pleaded with himself, but he could not resist.

Owen exited the boarding house in a murderous mood. He was about to mount his horse tied to the rail outside, when he saw Joshua approach. He turned away from the madman, pretending he had not noticed him. Owen was in no temperament for Joshua's mystical insights.

'Ssherriff! Ssherriff!' With slurred words, Joshua called over to Owen.

The lawman felt like punching a wall so strongly that his own fingers broke. Owen forcibly bit his own lip so that he did not explode in rage.

'Please, Joshua. I have to ride out immediately.' Owen knew that Joshua suffered from some kind of sickness of the head. The poor man could not control himself. Physical force would do nothing to remedy Joshua.

'You're in dangerr, Sherrrifff . . . I seen it in my visions . . . the angels told me . . . Dangerr . . . dangerr!'

'Thank you, Joshua,' Owen sullenly humoured the seer as he mounted his horse. Joshua's ravings would be comical, if Joshua himself was not such a tragic character.

'The beasts in the red mist . . . evil black eyes starin' out through the bloody fog . . . faces hidden by red!'

Even though Owen was now atop his roan, he could

41

still smell the air of alcohol hanging around Joshua. The sheriff cantered off for the long ride ahead of him.

'Take care, Joshua.'

Joshua carried on rambling as Owen rode away. The sheriff felt a pang of guilt at his brusqueness to Joshua, but only a pang. He had a lot to investigate and had no time for clairvoyant prophecies.

Inwardly, Joshua felt ashamed and embarrassed by his rant. Externally, he continued his psychic soliloquy. He could feel another vision rising, and was certain that Owen was in peril.

Tired and irritable, Owen set off for Saint Jude's. It would take the whole day to ride there and back, but the link to the goldmine was his only clue. Owen was strong-willed, and set his mind to the journey ahead. Though he felt as grumpy as a 'gator, he forced himself to concentrate on the ride. Owen had never visited Saint Jude's. The camp was highly secretive, though its men never bothered Prospect. He expected the miners to be on the defensive – if they even knew anything about the odd stranger at all.

Owen carried with him the red scarf from Renard's house. It was a plain item, and its possession by Renard may have been meaningless. Yet something in Joshua's unhinged monologue stuck with him. What did he mean by faces hidden by a red mist? It was an odd coincidence that Renard and the intruder both carried red bandanas. There was no possibility that Joshua could have known about the neckerchiefs. This was a detail that Owen had kept hidden, even from Elijah and Jeremiah. In Owen's experience, none of Brother Joshua's unworldly predictions had yet to come to pass. The sheriff thought no more of it as he rode on.

Nor did Owen detect the spying eyes watching him from the rocky hills.

CHAPTER 8

Karl was an expert in spying and stealth. He was astride his steed on the hilltop. Karl lit a cheroot, confident that there was enough distance between himself and the sheriff that Owen would not see the light, nor smell the cheap stink. The sun had risen and he had a perfect view of Owen in the foothills below. Karl's eyesight was outstanding. Though he was hundreds of feet away, he could see the details of Owen's face. Karl allowed himself to grin. The sheriff did not look happy.

As a young boy, he had been caught shoplifting in the drugstore. Helping himself to the candy seemed a daring ruse at the time, but his audacity was noticed. The shopkeeper had literally dragged Karl home by his ear. His mother had taken the strap to him, and beaten Karl's hide so powerfully that the boy could hardly walk. Karl had learned his lesson, though. Don't get caught.

From then on, Karl had planned his petty thefts with great care. He had used distraction techniques, highly practised sleight of hand, and at times even tricked his more stupid school friends into carrying out his bidding. Karl did not view himself as manipulative by nature. He merely saw theft and robbery as acts of survival. Though he was only twenty-two, Karl already saw the world as nothing but a mortal dogfight.

Karl favoured dark clothing. He was clad completely in black today. With his thick black moustache, Karl did indeed resemble a pantomime villain and his contemporaries had urged him to reconsider his garb. His striking appearance made it difficult to blend in and he was also highly attractive. He was not exactly charming (except when he needed to be), but quietly charismatic and commanding. People, and women especially, tended to remember Karl when he had been around.

Karl regarded his memorable appearance as an outward expression of his confidence, though. Whenever he organized a theft or a robbery, he made sure he was safely behind the scenes. He had yet to be arrested or tried for his prolific crimes. The authorities did not know his name, or even that he existed. Karl allowed his dancing puppets to answer to the lawmen.

The outlaw did not fear violence, nor apprehension, nor anything. In his early career, he had won the respect of his fellow criminals with his ruthlessness. When Karl killed, there were most certainly no witnesses left to describe the encounter.

Puffing on his cigar, Karl unhurriedly rode the stolen steed downhill. He was mindful of keeping the sheriff in sight, yet remaining unseen. As a leader of men – albeit lawless men – Karl nevertheless found that he carried out much of his work single-handedly. He had lieutenants that he trusted and confided in, yet most of his gang were a rabble. Karl saw them as mere pawns in the chess game he was winning. Moreover, Sheriff Rowlands was an unknown quantity. Prospect was relatively peaceful, and had yet to be raided by Karl's men. Naturally, Karl had sent scouts. They had reported that the sheriff was a schoolteacher, and a decent sort despite a bad temper. He was a smart guy, and good at talking people out of making trouble.

Karl was undecided as to the character of threat which Owen posed. A decent sort? Did that mean Owen would hunt a felon down, even if he was in danger? Or was it double-speak for being a coward?

The outlaw savoured his cheap cigar and the gentle undulations of his horse. The ocean blue sky was untouched by cloud. The pulsing sun would have forced another man to look away, but Karl thrived on its hellish rays. His black clothing only attracted more heat, and Karl revelled in it. He was much like a reptile warming itself on the rocks, in body and mind. Karl cherished things that others would call cheap and nasty. He was cunning and daring, yet no more ambitious than a rattlesnake. Unlike some of his cronies, Karl did have the intelligence to look ahead more than one day. He knew that the final chapter for him would be in the form of hanging, jail, or a bullet. But how long could he stay ahead of this fate? That was the game, for Karl.

He watched the dust from Owen's roan rise as it galloped through the desert below. The sandy cloud seemed to form an orange haze, much like a ball of flame. The cloud inched its way towards its destination. Leaving a trail in the sand below, Karl was reminded of the lit fuse of a stick of dynamite. As the spark on the fuse burned its way towards the explosive, it left the wire dead and black in its wake. Karl wondered if Owen would similarly leave the things he crossed dead and blackened.

It would be a long ride out to Saint Jude's, and Lord knows where Owen was headed next. Karl had been watching Owen from afar for the past day. The outlaw was not afraid to wait and watch a little longer. His vulture's patience was one of the characteristics that distinguished him from his lawless peers. Most of his gang could not think past their next beer. Like a chess player, Karl would wait and watch. He would learn what Owen had learned. And then he would make his move.

Karl lingered in the hills long enough for Owen to ride out of his sight. The swirl of sand disappeared over the horizon, vanishing like a candle light snuffed out. Karl spat out the cheroot. The outlaw knew with certainty that he could find the sheriff's trail. Indeed, he knew Owen's final destination in any case.

Karl reached into his breast pocket for his scarlet red scarf. He tied it around his face, and spurred his horse onwards.

CHAPTER 9

The miners saw Owen long before he arrived at their camp. The mine rarely received visitors. From time to time, fresh faces came to swell their numbers. Contemporaneously, the miners were killed in accidents and the Saint Jude population tended to remain steady.

The operation was a minor branch of a gold corporation in San Antonio. Saint Jude eked out a modest profit, so the company men did not interfere. Indeed, in their occasional visits, the business executives were welcomed politely, if not warmly. The company men always completed their business rapidly, and returned as soon as they could. They often felt an unspoken hostility in the air. Saint Jude's was not only a money-making undertaking. For its men, the mine was a refuge. Some were running away from something – often the law. Others were drifters with nobody, and nothing. Others still were outcasts, volatile individuals who were too mercurial for rising at dawn to milk cows, or sitting behind a counter. If they were not hacking away at rock, or blowing things up, they would be in jail.

The miners had been labouring since the early hours. It was Sunday, but Saint Jude did not follow the ordinary working calendar. It had its own rotas and rules which did not make provision for Sunday morning in church. As the sheriff came closer, most of the men were in the mine. A few were at its yawning entrance, maintaining equipment or resting. It was this handful who sighted Owen in the distance. Saint Jude was high in the rocky hills. Like a medieval fortress, they had an excellent view of approaching invaders.

Even visits from law officers were rare. When they sometimes travelled into Prospect, they were careful to avoid trouble. The men were a real mystery to outsiders. Though the men of Saint Jude were not angels, they obeyed an unexpressed set of rules. They worked together and lived together. Thefts and fights amongst the miners were unusual, and resolved with their own internal justice.

On one occasion, a miner had found that his tobacco pouch had disappeared. In their intimate community, it did not take long before the missing item was discovered in the pocket of a new face at the mine. The recruit said he was eighteen, but was probably only fifteen. He was a tough kid, and a hard worker. They needed boys like him. So the miners did not beat him, nor strap him. This lad was more than robust enough to shrug off a corporal punishment. Worse, they shunned him for a week. The boy could not join the miners in their meals. When he needed help with his work, he was blankly ignored. The once cocky grunt was soon reduced to helpless tears. The boy realized that he was only a cog in the Saint Jude machine. Without the support of his comrades, he was adrift.

They were not cruel men, and the young man was later accepted back into the fold. He had never erred since and was still with his comrades at the mine.

Looking over the cliff at the edge of the hill, they silently observed Owen draw near. The sheriff would have to ascend by a single rocky path to the main entrance. If the miners had any contraband to conceal, they would have had ample time. They had few possessions, though. As clannish as they were, Saint Jude had nothing illegal to hide. The miners lived a very simple, yet dangerous, life, for a few pennies and the opportunity to escape. They wondered if this unexpected guest would be a new recruit, or merely trouble. The men were hardy, and knew how to deal with troublemakers.

In the sands below, Owen began to climb the rocky track up to the main mine. During his journey, he had been wondering how to broach the subject. He had met miners from Saint Jude back in Prospect. While they were clearly rough diamonds, they were also respectful of the townsfolk and the law. The worst they ever did was get drunk and return to their hotel, before heading back out to the mine the next day. Their outward politeness was obviously a raised guard, though. These men did not want to get to know you, and did not want you to get to know them. Owen would have to manage his temper. Lord knows how the miners would react if Owen exploded in rage.

The roan gingerly climbed the path up into the rocky hills. Owen rocked back and forth uncomfortably in the saddle. Indeed, all day, Owen had had a nagging feeling that hidden eyes were following him. The sheriff would have to wear his best lawman's face. It could be unsettling, even for a sheriff, to be alone amongst a small army of tough miners. Sometimes, enforcing the law was just an act.

Arriving at the mine, Owen raised his hat respectfully. A few curious and stern-faced men had gathered around Owen's horse.

'Good mornin', gentlemen.' Owen dismounted. He knew they could clearly see his sheriff's badge. Yet the men were stony-faced. 'First of all, none of you's in any trouble. I just got a few questions 'bout a situation back in Prospect.' The miners did not break their concerted, impassive silence. Owen chose a man at random. None of them looked particularly friendly.

'Sir, back in Prospect, I chanced upon a most strange occurrence. Phillipe Renard is the retired schoolteacher of the town. I went to visit his home, and he was nowhere to be seen. He had vanished. His house was a real mess, but here's the weird thing. There was a stranger in the house, lying on Renard's bed. He was dyin' – taken a real beating. The stranger died just when I got there. Now, we did not know this individual back in Prospect. I have reason to believe he may have been working here at Saint Jude.'

This snippet of information caused an almost imperceptible stir. The miners tried to maintain their rocky demeanours. Owen, though, noticed knowing, glancing eyes.

A voice from an older man, possibly one of the odd community's elders, drew Owen's attention.

'Sheriff, come an' talk to me 'bout that. I know the man you're talking about.'

CHAPTER 10

Mordecai was the de facto leader of Saint Jude, not that the miners held elections or votes. His years in the mine had etched wrinkles and cracks on his face. He wore a dirty white beard. Yet he was also lean, strong and mentally sharp. Owen could not place his age, he could have been anywhere between forty and seventy. Mordecai was a little shorter than Owen. The miners' leader was not an imposing figure, yet his men clearly deferred to him.

In his native Florida, Mordecai had been a builder. It was not a need to escape the noose that had driven him to Saint Jude. Rather, Mordecai had absconded out of shame.

Having completed his apprenticeship, Mordecai had wed when he was a very young man. For a short time, he and his teenage bride had lived together in what Mordecai falsely thought was bliss. An excellent construction man, Mordecai was never idle. He had been well paid for his skills with the hammer and the trowel. After a strenuous day in the sun, Mordecai adored returning home to his beautiful young wife. Before long, he thought he had fathered a baby son. The boy had been born with a shock of blond hair. As a young man, Mordecai's own hair was an inky black. Mordecai chose not to dwell on this incongruity: it was common for babies to be born blonde, and their hair to darken with age.

Retrospectively, Mordecai was forcibly ignoring the truth. As the months went on, and the boy's features became more and more clear, the lack of resemblance to Mordecai began to bother him.

He found he could not confront his wife Magda about the question. Rather, he commented on the missing similarities in an indirect way. Magda would cruelly turn these insinuations into a joke. Laughing in Mordecai's face, she would mockingly hint at her infidelities.

'You think he's another man's child? Come on, now, Mordecai. You're more than man enough for me!'

Magda had been a wild and wilful young girl, and devastatingly attractive. That had been her great appeal. The boys had all loved her, and when she agreed to take Mordecai's hand, he felt that he had won a prize. Magda, too, secretly felt that she had won big. She would be provided for by a decent, hard-working builder – and when the dupe was looking the other way, she would do whatever the heck she liked!

Only a year into their marriage, Mordecai was seeing that explosive allure from another angle. More and more, Magda's spiteful taunts made Mordecai feel impotent and pathetic. Moreover, Magda was spurning Mordecai's approaches in the bedroom.

When he took to spying on their home, Mordecai was disgusted to learn that Magda indeed received a gentleman caller. Mordecai did not recognize the man. As his cuckolded surveillance continued, Mordecai soon found that there were other male visitors on other days. Mordecai did not feel a need to commit murder, nor scream out his new knowledge to his unfaithful wife. He only felt weakened and deflated. Mordecai had had great hopes for the little boy who was plainly not his son. He also began to realize that he was something of a joke in the town. It seemed to Mordecai that everybody knew, except him.

Mordecai felt resigned, rather than enraged. He suddenly knew what to do. There would be no profit from beating Magda, or worse. She would be left to raise her bastard alone. Mordecai suspected that her lovers would not be financially supportive: he sure as heck was not going to be bringing up that boy. One day, Mordecai had packed his things away and walked out. Naturally, Magda unleashed an earful of stinging remarks, but they only served to satisfy Mordecai. She never thought he would abandon her, yet walk out he did.

Though he tried not to look back, Mordecai remembered with clarity Magda's jilted teasing whilst her baby screamed in the background. He had felt ashamed that he had been deceived, yet equally guilty that he was leaving the two of them to their shameful fate.

Mordecai had drifted for years, picking up building work here and there. While he was glad that the harlot was out of his life, he found he had no appetite to wed again. Mordecai found that Saint Jude was the sanctuary he needed. His fellow miners did not ask too many questions about his sullied history. The gold mine was a refuge for men without a past.

*

Mordecai led Owen to his private tent, erected a few minutes' walk from the entrance. It was a large construction, as big as Owen's boarding room. The air in the tent was dirty and stifling. Owen realized that Mordecai lived here year after year. The miner invited the sheriff to sit at a table inside the tent. Mordecai began to brew some coffee on a simple camping fire. The old man – if he was all that old – was saying nothing. Though he felt awkward and uncomfortable, Owen broke the silence.

'I sure appreciate you taking the time to speak to me, sir. If I'm not imposin', will you tell me some about your own story?' Owen wondered if he was prying. He wanted to learn as much about the situation as he could.

Mordecai did not like this particular intrusion. 'I been minin' here some twenty years, Sheriff. Come from Florida, originally. Respectfully, Sheriff, that's all you need to know. Nobody here been breakin' no laws, Officer. I'm happy to talk, but the men here are . . .' He paused to consider the right phrase. '. . .very private.'

'Thank you, Mordecai. Please tell me about the stranger I'm lookin' into.'

Mordecai gave an exasperated sigh, as though he were about to describe an errant son. 'Sheriff, it's well known what goes on at Saint Jude. I mean – the job we do in the grand scheme of things. Minin' is a dirty, dangerous job. Explosions, collapses, floods – or just plain ol' exhaustion from the heat. It's not work for everyone – especially out here in the middle o' nowhere. The men who come here are runaways. Not out and out crooks. We're kinda a sanctuary for waifs and strays. And, surely enough, we git some crazy ones.'

Pausing again, Mordecai poured two cups of coffee into two tin mugs. They could have used a wash, but Owen sipped on the scalding drink politely.

'They don't normally stick around long. Mining is not an occupation for the kinda man who can't sit still for five minutes. A few weeks ago, one such crazy man showed up lookin' for work. He was a young kid, maybe eighteen or nineteen. He looked Mexican or Indian, but he spoke English like a white man. Said his name was Arthur – but that may well be a fake name. We gave him a chance. We'll give anyone a chance.'

Mordecai took a mouthful of coffee and continued.

'Arthur was a damned lunatic. He wasn't a bad kid. He worked hard, and he never started no fights, nor stole nothin'. But he was trouble. The way he acted – he rubbed the men up the wrong way. Arthur could be silent for hours, then he'd do something or see something he found interesting. Then, he'd go on and on and on and on. He really did try the patience of us all. There was this one time, Arthur was down the shaft, excavating away. At the end of his shift, another man went to switch with him. Now this other guy only had one ear. I don't know why – it's his business. But Arthur couldn't resist. Even though Arthur's stretch was over, he pestered and pestered this other guy. He tried to be friendly and polite, but in the end Arthur was too much. There was a stand-off, but the other men broke it up.'

Owen was fascinated. Was this the same man at Renard's house?

'It was like that over and over again with Arthur. At

56

Saint Jude, we hate to throw anyone out. We ain't no prep school. But this boy Arthur was nuts. He also had a thing about dynamite. Now, there was no way I would let the boy near no explosives. But whenever we used dynamite, Arthur stuck to us like glue. He loved the stuff, and he was always interferin'. We caught him playing around with the dynamite sticks a few times. He got so excitable. The crazy thing was, I think he'd used dynamite before. Questions he asked, and comments he made – it was like he really was familiar with dynamite.

'Now, it was getting to the point where I was gonna run Arthur off the camp. But then – a couple of nights ago – he just upped and left. He was not in his tent in the morning. He didn't steal a horse or nothing, and nobody saw him leave. I don't know for sure, but he sounds a lot like the boy you found in this Renard's house.'

The sheriff nodded attentively. His coffee was barely touched, but Mordecai had drained his.

'Is there anything else you can tell me about this Arthur character?'

'He liked to tell tall tales – and I mean real make-believe stuff. He said a few times that he was a Roman soldier, and sometimes that he was in an outlaw gang. Even though they were just fairy tales, it was the way he described his stories. Arthur could read and write, and it seemed to me that he had had a lot of book learning.

'He really wasn't a bad kid. I wish I could have straightened him out. But Arthur was too much.'

As Owen left Saint Jude, he thanked Mordecai for his time with a firm handshake. The mining foreman had been helpful, yet Owen could sense that Mordecai was glad to see him leaving.

The sheriff had another long ride ahead.

Unseen, Karl continued his vigil.

CHAPTER 11

Owen rode on. He was pleased that he had learned something about Arthur's background. Nevertheless, as interesting as the account by the mining foreman was, it did not lead him any closer to Renard. Owen hoped that perhaps he could pick up more information along the way. His next stop was in Blackwood, in Brecon County. Owen would call in on this Aunt Jasmine character.

Blackwood was another fifty or so miles' ride north. It would take a few hours. At another time, Owen would have enjoyed the respite from both teaching and enforcing the law. Today, though, the journey loomed ahead of the sheriff like an endless tunnel. The burden of the investigation ahead of him weighed on Owen. He could ride and ride all day, hunt down Aunt Jasmine, yet still learn nothing.

Though the sheriff knew his way with great accuracy, the flat desert around him seemed to be goading him. Behind every rocky outcrop or mesa, Owen sensed menace. For a moment, he wondered if he had made the correct decision by riding out alone. His lawman's instinct was tingling. Out there, somewhere, was a threat.

Owen could handle bandits or rustlers. What bothered Owen, though, was that he was up against a totally unknown enemy.

Though the heat haze was particularly dazzling, the sheriff pressed on. The cruel gaze of the noon sun stung. The only thing for it was to keep his mind on the ride ahead. Like many of the other men in Prospect, Owen was an individual of impassable tenacity and determination. Little matter the shirt soaked with perspiration, nor the burning heat radiating from the skies. Renard was out there somewhere, and he was depending on Owen.

Blackwood was a small town, larger than Prospect, of perhaps a few hundred souls. It was prosperous for the region, though much of its wealth was derived from gambling and alcohol. The settlement had a lively reputation as a good time place. Young men from Prospect and other towns would journey to Blackwood for a little adventure, away from their parents and wives.

As Owen approached in the late afternoon, he felt no aura of conviviality. In the distance, Blackwood only looked shadowy and foreboding. He could see a few individuals walking up and down the streets, though they looked as small and insignificant as ants. The town appeared as though it were a gloomy island in a hostile sea of sand. Owen wondered what kind of reception Blackwood would demonstrate. The prickle of the sun had made Owen irritable, and he would not suffer any drunk fools gladly.

Riding down the main street, though, Owen found that the party town was hungover. Only a handful of locals were going about their business. Indeed, it was Sunday afternoon. He did not seem to be drawing a lot of attention to himself. Owen figured that Blackwood was used to strangers coming and going all the time. He could hear a little bustle coming from the saloon, though. He had Jasmine's address from her letter to Renard, but it would do no harm to ask around. Owen was also parched after his thirsty ride.

After dismounting and tying his roan to the rail, Owen swung through the batwing doors of the tavern. The cool shade was a welcome reprieve. There were only a few drinkers, and Owen was glad that they did not pay him any mind. At the bar, Owen asked for a jug of water. He longed for a beer, but he was not willing to impair his judgement, even slightly. The barman was a dark-haired fellow with jet black hair and a droopy moustache. He grinned jovially with blackened teeth as he served Owen.

'Here you go, Sheriff. No charge just for water. Anything else I can help you with?' The barkeeper was no doubt accustomed to strangers, although Owen detected a hint of curiosity as to why a lawman was in town.

'Partner, I'm looking for a friend of a friend. Her address is on Sunnyside Street. Her name is. . . .'

The barman's laughter interrupted Owen.

'You ain't after Jasmine Renard, is you, Sheriff?' Owen felt a brief spike of anger not to be included in the bar-keeper's little joke, but managed to keep his cool. The barman continued.

'Jasmine Renard has lots of gentleman admirers. Least she says she does! Nice to finally meet one in the flesh.' From Jasmine's letter, Owen imagined that Jasmine was no saint. He slid a dollar bill across the counter.

'Here's what I owe you for the water. Anything else

you can tell me about this Jasmine Renard?'

'Jasmine's down here every night. No doubt she's sleeping off her hangover this afternoon, and she'll be back in the saloon in an hour or two. She's fifty, maybe even sixty. She might have been a looker in her day, but now – well, she does try. No husband, no family, no job. Don't know how she makes ends meet, but she's always got money for a drink. She been here in Blackwood as long as I remember. Some say she's connected to a rich East Coast family.'

Owen thanked the barkeeper, and asked for directions to Sunnyside Street. The sheriff gulped the water. Just as he was about to set off, the barman added some further advice.

'Sheriff, Jasmine would most certainly appreciate a bottle of whiskey. A little drink's gonna loosen her tongue.'

A few moments later, with a cheap bottle of whiskey under his arm, Owen knocked on Jasmine's door. He could hear some coughing, something breaking, and heavy, uneven footsteps. As the door opened, Owen was struck by the nauseous air of stale alcohol and decay.

The wreck of a woman that answered was clad in a filthy, low-cut dress. Her face was so hideously smudged by makeup that she resembled an unearthly circus clown. Before Owen could speak, the crone smiled toothlessly.

'You looking for Phillipe Renard, Sheriff?'

CHAPTER 12

Before Owen could answer, the hag snatched the whiskey bottle from him and returned to her room. Owen followed her, as she began pouring the whiskey into a filthy shot glass. Jasmine lived in a single chamber. Her little apartment was repellently dirty. There were bedsheets and clothes piled ankle high on the floor, and a makeshift bed with no sheets. On a table pushed against the far wall were pieces of rotten food, which were now feasts for maggots and flies. The smell was unsettlingly disgusting. Owen had to apply much willpower to contain his stomach contents.

'Ma'am, I am indeed looking for Phillipe Renard. What can you tell me about him? Are you aware what's happened to him?' The sheriff may have felt some pity for the old witch, were it not for the air of evil emanating from the creature. Nevertheless, Owen knew he had to be polite.

'Siddown, Sheriff.'

Jasmine conjured a couple of stools, which – in contrast to the room's other contents – looked sturdy and strong. Owen sat courteously, feeling something sticky at the back of his pants.

'I used to be a showgirl in Paris, you know, Officer.' She began to jiggle her hips as she took another shot of whiskey.

'Please, ma'am. Phillipe Renard went missing yesterday. He has no family in Prospect. Amongst his things, I discovered a letter from you to Renard. Are you related to him?'

Knocking back another shot, Jasmine settled down on her stool.

'You know why Phillipe Renard came out West?'

'No, ma'am. Phillipe was always very private about his family background.'

'Because he was diss-graced, Sheriff. Diss-graced!' Jasmine's eyes flared insanely, and she continued drunkenly. 'Phillipe's daddy – my brother – was named Clement. He was in charge of the family money. He was no family man. Phillipe's mama died giving birth to him. No other children. Sure, Phillipe's daddy paid for private tuition and prep school, but he had no time for Phillipe. Clement was always a million miles away. Not travelling, or such like. I mean up here.'

She laid a gnarled finger on her temple. 'Course, I tried to help, but Clement wasn't having it. Said he wasn't having no showgirl looking after his boy. So I never saw much of Phillipe growing up.'

For a moment, Jasmine seemed saddened.

'Now he was a smart one, young Phillipe. Even though Daddy wasn't interested, he was a good student. Top of the class. Full of it, too. Downright arrogant. He always talked about European philosophers and such like.

Phillipe got in trouble, too. Drinking, whoring, fighting. Never learned, though. His daddy bailed him out, or paid people off. Anything for a quiet life. So Phillipe never changed.'

Owen wondered how much of Jasmine's tale was pure invention. This description sounded so unlike Renard.

'Then it went too far. I heard Renard fathered a child out of wedlock. Now, there was no running away from this. Round the same time, Clement up and died. Craziest situation. Clement was in good health, but died in his sleep. Now Phillipe was in charge of the family money. Varmint cut me off and got the hell out of town. That was near on twenty years ago.'

Slugging more whiskey, she smiled with false humour. 'Course, we all know what really occurred. Phillipe poisoned his own daddy. He was smart enough to make it look all natural, like. Now he had all the money. With no money and no husband, I danced my way out West. Not much left from my inheritance.'

'What happened to the woman who was with child?'

'No idea, Sheriff. Sure thing, Phillipe was glad to get away from her. He was no daddy in the making.'

Owen explained the circumstances of Renard's disappearance, but by now Jasmine did not appear to be listening. She was only interested in more whiskey, and much of the bottle had already been consumed. Jasmine grunted incoherent answers in response to the sheriff's questions. Owen was disconcerted by the woman's apparent lack of interest in the crime. Again, he wondered if her story was true. Renard was so erudite and distinguished, yet incongruously related to the hag sat before him.

'I am grateful for your time and information, ma'am. Before I leave, I do have one more question. Who would want to hurt Renard? What enemies did he have?'

'Back East – jealous husbands, gambling debts, any poor kid Renard beat the hell out of. Lots of enemies. No big surprise he ran away. Didn't care no two hoots 'bout Aunty Jasmine.'

Thanking Jasmine, Owen was glad to leave her little dungeon. He felt like scrubbing himself with a wire brush. The pure air outside was a sweet relief.

Owen wondered why Renard had always kept Jasmine secret. Was his learned friend embarrassed by his ship-wreck of a relation – or was Renard concealing darker mysteries? The sheriff would have much to digest as he rode back to Prospect. Despite the day's interesting encounters, nothing had been revealed that advanced Owen closer to a resolution. Perhaps he should send out search parties, he wondered.

As Owen mounted his horse for the ride home, he asked himself what on earth he was going to do next. Renard's disappearance was obviously no ordinary abduction. Indeed, Owen reflected, whenever he had been stuck on a case, it was usually Renard's brain that Owen picked first.

It was late afternoon. The sun was beginning to sink, though its fiery blaze had not diminished. The ground grew more shadowy, and – though it was Sunday evening – a few revellers appeared, like ghouls rising from their crypts. Owen could not share in Blackwood's merriment. To him, the town had the aura of a funeral wake. He was glad to be setting off.

Jasmine herself was about to join in the evening's

revelry at the saloon, when a knock on her door signalled the arrival of another unexpected visitor.

CHAPTER 13

Jasmine had rather enjoyed entertaining Sheriff Rowlands. He was a polite and respectful young man. Good looking, too. She wondered what fanciful stories she could tell her friends down at the saloon. No doubt they would be curious about Jasmine's handsome gentleman caller. Owen's generosity with the whiskey bottle had only added to the day's pleasure. The bottle was not quite empty yet, and Jasmine was in the mood for a couple more drinks.

The old woman had lied to herself and others so often and so badly that she was no longer certain what the reality was. Her yarns were, like her drinking, an artificial way of insulating herself from her painful loneliness. Jasmine's account of Phillipe's past had largely been correct: she had been much younger, and soberer, then. Her memories of that time had not yet been fractured by whiskey.

There was one thing that she did not mention to Owen, that she had not thought on in a while: her fear of Phillipe. He had been more than merely a cocksure young scoundrel. Her own nephew had grown to make her feel uncomfortable by his mere presence. She had already drunkenly forgotten her letter to Phillipe. However, she was now beginning to recall the sense of menace which he emanated. Suddenly, she was glad that Phillipe was far away.

Though she did not realize it, Jasmine did in fact receive a meagre income from her family's investments. The small pension was paid directly into her bank account. It was a pittance, but the few pennies paid for the rent of her pigsty. For years, she did in fact work as a dancer, drifting from town to town towards the West. Despite her empty boast to Owen, she had never even been to Paris and would not be able to find it on a map. Her ageing and excessive imbibing had brought her career as a showgirl to an end.

Since then, she had done odd jobs, mooched, exchanged favours with men, and ended up in Blackwood. Jasmine had been there for a few years, but could not remember exactly how many. She had grown into the role of one of the town's characters. Jasmine was viewed as the vampish mature lady who could still create chemistry with much younger men. At least, she had told herself this many, many times. As destructive as her drinking was, Jasmine was not totally delusional. A little bit of her knew that she was a standing joke in the town, and even an object of pity.

Still, it had been an enjoyable afternoon. Jasmine sat back and enjoyed the view from her unwashed window. The sun had left, and the sky was clear. Slugging the dregs of whiskey directly from the bottle, Jasmine lost herself staring up at the stars. Like her mind, the heavenly bodies were far, far removed from the earth. It was a beautiful night, the skies an inky, velvet black. Rapt, Jasmine felt serene as she gazed at the stars. For a few moments, she thought of nothing at all. Her mind was peacefully restful.

Her trance did not last long. Her consumption of the last drops of whiskey broke her reverie. It was hardly sundown, yet Jasmine had drunk an entire bottle and was ready for a few more drinks. Staggering, Jasmine rose to make herself pretty for the boys at the bar. Like a coyote rummaging in trash, she dug through the mounds of clothing until she selected the right attire. Jasmine would wear a ripped, green, low cut dress that had never, ever been washed. She was about to get changed, when there was a knock on the door.

Outside, Karl had timed his strike expertly. There were a few individuals around, but Karl made certain that he rapped on the old woman's door during an instant when there were no witnesses. He knew very little about the pathetic harridan inside, but she needed to be silenced. There would be no need to sweet-talk his way into her pit. Karl would address the situation ruthlessly. The only reason he did not kick the door open was to prevent the sound from attracting attention.

Jasmine opened the door. Her final thoughts were that the man outside looked familiar. Though half his face was masked by a red bandana, she believed she recognized her assassin's intense dark eyes. Jasmine did not have the opportunity to speak, though.

Karl pounced like a scorpion. Jasmine was an old, intoxicated woman but Karl was an experienced killer. He knew that the actions of a human in its death throes were unpredictable. Karl pushed past Jasmine and trapped her neck in his arm from behind her. Dragging her back into her unkempt den, he closed the door behind him with his foot. Jasmine began to wriggle like a swine, but Karl's deadly embrace gripped like a steel mantrap. Before Jasmine could scream or moan, Karl pressed his hand over her mouth. The killer tightened his grip, masterfully controlling Jasmine's desperate writhes and kicks.

The shock of the assault had sobered Jasmine in an instant. Though she thrashed with the might of ten women, her twists and turns were countered by the killer's lethal hold. She was ironically clearheaded in her terminal moments. Jasmine wondered – despite her terrified confusion – where she had encountered her assailant before.

As close to Jasmine as a lover, Karl intimately inhaled the crone's foul odours. Amongst the chemical smell of alcohol and the dirty stink of lingering sweat, Karl detected the perfume of fear. This aroma was a narcotic to him, and it energized him to complete his murderous task. When Jasmine grew floppy in his arms, he carried on crushing her neck a little longer. Just to be certain.

CHAPTER 14

Leaving Blackwood, Owen decided to follow the trail through the rocky hills. He would have been confident retracing his route homeward through the desert. However, his lawman's sense of danger was still prickling. Indeed, Owen's feeling of dread was almost palpable. He felt that the desert was no place to be tonight.

The trail was well-lit under a serene moon, and the air was comfortably warm. On another occasion, it would have been a very pleasant evening. The sheriff, though, thought he saw movement in every shadow, and a face behind every rock. Curiously, Owen remembered Brother Joshua's apparent prophecy. The madman's words played on his mind. Owen was not the nervous type, yet his unease tonight was almost painful. The ride ahead loomed like an agonizing and unforgiving task.

Less than a mile behind him, Karl stalked his quarry. The tranquil moon supplied ample illumination from its silver stare. However, Karl had well-developed night vision. The sheriff was not going to escape his hunter's eyesight. Like a ghost, he had murdered Jasmine and stolen away without being detected. Though he was still excited by his killing of the old woman, Karl was not a man to let his passions rule his reason. He needed to be composed for his next attack. With measured haste, Karl's horse was catching up with Owen's.

Owen's anxiety spiked sickeningly when he heard hoofbeats behind him. They were not galloping, and the sound could easily have been missed in the eerie silence. The sheriff's senses were magnified, though, and he was anticipating menace at any instant. He withdrew his Colt from its holster and cocked it.

Karl was listening intently in the distance, and detected the sound of Owen's Colt being readied. He withdrew his own weapon. The killer was greatly thrilled at the prospect of his next assault, yet he restrained himself. Gaining unseen on the sheriff, Karl would know when the time was right.

Owen could hear the hoofbeats drawing closer, and spurred his roan onwards. He also heard his predator's horse accelerate, and now he was in no doubt. Owen was being chased. Looking back behind him as he dashed away, Owen could see a stirring in the shadows. In the darkness, Owen noticed a silver metallic flash and then the report of gunfire. The lawman was not so much terrified as desperate to survive, a cornered wild animal. With one hand on the reins, Owen stretched around to blindly fire his weapon in response.

Karl was still hidden in the gloom, but close enough to observe Owen's actions. As the lawman shot back, Karl did not stir. This was because of a mixture of arrogant fearlessness and pure experience of killing. Karl could practically see in the dark, so accustomed was he to stealth and murder. Owen, however, was shooting sight-lessly. Karl had the time and composure to cock his six shooter again for its next shot. Owen would not be able to blindly prepare his weapon for the next round. The killer knew that Owen was an experienced lawman – if only a part-time one. The sheriff was making errors because he was frightened. This was something that Karl intended to cruelly exploit.

He spurred his own horse onwards. A strong horse-man and tracker, Karl was not worried about Owen getting away. The murderer merely wanted to panic the sheriff, and see the worry in his face as he drew closer. When Karl was a few feet away, he felt like a shark trap-ping a wounded fish. Owen's visage was ghostly and terrified in the moonlight.

Still darting his head back and forth as he rode, Owen now had a much better view of his stalker. The individual was clad only in black, though the mask around his face seemed to be red. Owen did not presently have the opportunity to dwell on the significance of the crimson scarf, though. He was fearfully riding hard, frantic to steal away from the phantom on his trail.

The killer was very near now, near enough to land a well-aimed shot. Owen could almost feel the hand of death on his shoulder. He was hardly somebody with nothing to lose. Owen had a beautiful girl, a career he loved and had commanded the respect of his townsfolk as their law enforcer. No, it was not a question of having nothing to lose. Owen was simply not a coward and was not willing to die like a mouse in the claws of a cat.

The sheriff yanked hard on the reins, bringing his roan to a screaming halt. The horse raised itself on its

74

hind legs. With breathless audacity, he fired his next shot at his chaser.

As Owen's roan stopped unexpectedly, Karl's horse was forced to halt. It, too, rose up on its back legs. Karl was thrown from the animal, and landed painfully on the rocky ground. The killer received a knock on the head, and was dazed for a second. It was all the time Owen needed. Owen dismounted rapidly, and seized Karl's lapels as he lay prone on the ground.

The sheriff's bad temper had been a lifelong challenge for him. Fiery and mercurial as a child, his parents' discipline – as well as Renard's gentle guidance – had helped him to master his simmering rage. Though he was no priest, Owen had learned how to subjugate his own anger.

The constant testing by his schoolchildren, and the ordeals of administering justice, had been trying. There were occasions when Owen had exploded, and had later regretted his outburst of rage. There had been certain times that he had been so angry with the idiotic drunks and petty crooks that he policed that Elijah or Jeremiah had had to reel Owen in.

Unfortunately for Karl, Owen's deputies were not present to arbitrate tonight. Owen's furious fists rained down on Karl like the paws of a rabid ape.

CHAPTER 15

Still dazed from his fall, Karl was too disorientated to fight back. Owen struck blow after punishing blow. He was a powerfully built man. His angry strikes bloodied and bruised Karl's face. The sheriff pummelled with such ferocity that after a few moments, he was breathless. He stopped for a second to snatch the red kerchief away from Karl's face. This instant was the only respite Karl needed.

As Owen motioned to seize the bandana, Karl grasped the lawman's wrist. Pulling on Owen's arm with one hand, and clutching Owen's back with the other, Karl deftly wrestled the sheriff away. He switched places with the sheriff in a crocodile roll. Karl's gun had been thrown out of his hand during his fall from horseback. His only opportunity now was to eradicate the lawman using his empty hands alone.

Like a lightning flash, Karl's hands were around Owen's throat. His fingers gripped Owen's neck like the devil. Karl's hands tightened and tightened.

'Get out of this, Sheriff,' spat Karl with venom in his voice.

Whereas Karl was an accomplished murderer, Owen had no such clever techniques. The sheriff's instinct was to grab Karl's wrists and push his throttling embrace away. Owen knew that this would fail, though. Karl's grasp was too potent. The killer recoiled, as much from surprise as from pain, when Owen cruelly inserted his finger into Karl's eye. He cried out, releasing the lawman and staggering to his feet. Though Owen had no idea who his assailant was, the attacker looked almost comical as he swayed clumsily, holding his hand to his eye. The sheriff did not have time to giggle, though. He leapt to his feet, and kicked away Karl's gun into the darkness. Owen had been mindful to holster his own weapon before halting his horse. He now drew the gun, and cocked it.

'Stranger, you ain't going no place. Put your hands in the air. I'll shoot if I have to.'

Karl reluctantly raised his arms, despite his throbbing eye. He viewed the scuffle with Owen as no more than a minor irritation. Karl found it amusing that Owen had bettered him in this way. He would cooperate for now, if only to play for time. Karl did not fear a violent death, and saw it as simply part of the game.

'Take off your mask.'

Karl was not happy about this. He had always been careful to remain in the shadows during his outlaw career. Karl was particular who he revealed himself to, and was not keen to expose himself to a lawman. Nevertheless, Karl went along with it. This meant that he would most certainly have to kill Owen later on, though.

Karl undid the knot at the back of his neck, and allowed the scarf to fall away. Owen was interested to see who his mystery attacker was. The stranger had ruddy, sharp features and a thick black moustache. Young, maybe twenty-two. Owen did not recognize him.

'Now talk.'

Though the stranger's nose was bloody, and his face was covered by ugly red welts that would soon be colourful bruises, he smiled arrogantly. At once, Owen could tell that he was dealing with one conceited individual.

'Sheriff, as you know, I ain't gonna tell you nothing. You can beat me, shoot me, march me off to jail. But I ain't talking.'

'Give me your name.'

Karl laughed vainly. 'I could tell you, Sheriff. How would you know if I was telling the truth?'

The stranger's vanity was aggravating Owen, who was already riled. He would have to be careful not to lose it. Owen took a pace closer to Karl and pointed the gun at his skull. The killer seemed unperturbed, even amused. His mocking smile did not wane.

'We know all about you, Sheriff. You ain't gonna shoot me dead. You're the decent, stand-up type. Not gonna shoot a man who can't shoot back.'

The killer's barb provoked a pulse of anger in Owen. True enough, Owen was not in the business of shooting unarmed men. This character, though, was testing him. He needed to assert control of the situation.

'Stranger, if you resist, I will use lethal force. Turn around and face away from me. Put your hands behind your back. I'm gonna cuff you.'

The stranger obeyed, although Owen had the inkling that the killer was only playfully going through the motions to irk him. Owen attached the manacles a little too tightly.

'Now I'm gonna march you back to Prospect. I'll ride, and you'll be on foot. It's gonna be a long night for you. If you run, I will fire on you. Any dirty tricks, and I will shoot.'

'Yes, sir!' chirped Karl.

Owen mounted his roan.

'Move it!'

As they set off, Owen began to dread the journey ahead of him. Riding at the same pace as the killer, the passage would take all night. Owen would have to be constantly alert, as well. His charge was as deadly and slippery as a snake.

Karl, however, was secretly enjoying every second of his encounter. He now had a good measure of Owen. The sheriff was no gentleman lawman. Owen was ready to fight when pressed. Indeed, the sheriff had somehow won the upper hand over him. Karl wasted so much of his time with small time crooks who were not one tenth of the man he was. He was glad of the contest which Owen was supplying. The sheriff had most certainly earned Karl's admiration. It was going to be a shame to kill him.

In the darkness, Owen could not see Karl's hands fidgeting with the handcuffs. Karl had developed such skill in escaping from irons that he could manipulate the manacles without creating any sound. He was not picking the lock: Karl had slyly taken the keys from Owen's belt.

As Karl raced away, his hands freed, he was confident that Owen's gunshots would not strike him as he disappeared back into the shadows.

Owen emptied his revolver, cursing himself and the enigmatic stranger.

Something the killer had said haunted Owen as he returned to Prospect.

'We know all about you, Sheriff.'

'We?'

CHAPTER 16

Riding hard, Owen arrived back in Prospect in good time. He spurred his roan on furiously, trying – and failing – not to dwell on the frustrations of his investigation. He had learned nothing useful. He had been told a few things about the stranger at the gold mine, and some suspect stories about Renard's past. However, these revelations only deepened the mystery. Owen still lacked any inkling of Renard's whereabouts.

The sheriff was also angry with himself. He had nearly been murdered by the black-clad killer, and somehow allowed the outlaw to abscond. Owen had realized that the keys to his cuffs were missing from his belt. He had no idea how the assassin had succeeded in sneaking away the keys. Owen tried to reassure himself that the killer was clearly an expert footpad. That thought, though, only worried him more. It showed how near to death the sheriff had come.

Owen was thankful to see Prospect in the distance. The town looked tranquil under the stars and the silvery moon. Owen hoped that he would find some sanctuary for the rest of the night. He directed himself straight to the Boltons' farm house. The sheriff felt a twinge of guilt that he would be stirring the family from their rest. However, when they knew what had happened, they would understand.

Pa Bolton welcomed Owen in, dressed in his bed-clothes. He woke his wife and daughter, and set to making some coffee on the stove.

'Son, what the hell happened to you? Dear God, I'm glad you're all right. Sit down, son, and rest some.'

As Ma Bolton and Mary fretted over him, Owen was so humbled that he felt close to tears. He would never forget how lucky he was to be cared about by such kind people.

Mary filled a pan with water, and began mopping Owen's face. Though he came away from the encounter in a better state than his opponent, Owen was scratched and bruised. He did not realize how pale he appeared, from fear and exhaustion. Though they did not press him, Owen shared his experiences with the family. They were moved and shocked by the events. Owen was dear to them, and the Boltons were alarmed by what had happened.

'Son, tonight you stay here with us. No polite excuses. And damn any wagging tongues! We ain't got no spare room, but you can bed down here in the main room. Or shack up with us two.'

Pa Bolton left it unsaid that Owen would not be sharing Mary's bed. Merely allowing Owen to stay was a great act of kindness, though. If an inquisitive neighbour noticed Owen leaving the house on the morrow, there would indeed be spicy rumours.

'Thank you, Pa. I'll bed down here in the parlour.

You're most kind, Pa.'

'You did the right thing coming here, Sheriff. We care for you. Now get some sleep.' Ma and Pa left Owen with Mary, though he knew he could not keep her from her bed for too long.

They embraced. Owen lost himself in the warmth of his sweetheart's breast. For an instant, he forgot all about Renard and the feeling of being stalked. Owen concentrated purely on his love for the young woman who cherished him so deeply. The instants were only fleeting.

'Owen, honey, I'm so glad you're safe. I don't know what I'd do if I lost you.'

'There, now, Mary. Don't talk like that.' Owen reassured her courageously, though he knew his words were without conviction. Never had he faced the peril he currently did. He did not truly know the nature of his foe.

'You're a brave man, Owen. You don't have to face this alone. Elijah and Jeremiah will back you up. Hell, you can deputize every man in Prospect. We really don't know what we're up against here.'

Mary did not ask Owen to resign as sheriff, nor run away. She never would. He was a devoted man. His schoolchildren and his townsfolk respected him. Though they might not have realized it, the whole town depended on him. Mary Bolton did not fall in love with a fraidy-cat.

Owen had no answer. They rested their heads together silently, forehead to forehead. Even in the dying light, Mary was strikingly beautiful. The shadows gave her an ethereal and angelic appearance. Not even the darkness could mask the gentleness and dedication that shone in her eyes.

In truth, Owen was not certain what to do next. With Mary, though, he did not have to force a pretence of authority. A man had to be strong, but with his girl he was not afraid to bare his fears.

'I don't think I've ever been so afraid, Mary. If I hadn't been lucky tonight, that stranger could've finished me. It's been so strange round here the past two days. It's like there's someone out there, watching and waiting. Does that sound crazy?'

'No, sweetheart. You're right. It's so odd what happened to Renard. I know you, though. You won't let your friend down. And you're safe here.' Tenderly, she kissed his brow. Though he had been inside a while and had imbibed a little coffee, his skin was cold and white.

The fire in the hearth was fading, and the room was cooling. There was only the slightest flicker from the flames. The darkness and the cold began to make Owen feel deflated. He drew Mary closer. Her warmth – both from her body, and the warmness that emanated from her soul – strengthened him. Their love was a potent reminder that there was something worth fighting for. He prayed that this would not be his last night in her arms.

Alone with his girl, Owen did not have to restrain his emotion anymore. He buried his head in her shoulder, and wept.

CHAPTER 17

Confiding in Mary had given Owen vigour. He and the Boltons awoke at sunrise, and the sheriff had slept well. Owen found that he was filled with energy. He had had a few thoughts about his next steps. Over breakfast, the sheriff was talkative and lively. Owen understood that it was the support of Mary and her parents that had invigorated him. He truly counted himself fortunate that they were by his side.

Setting off through the door, Owen kissed Mary on the cheek and didn't give a damn who saw it. She blushed like a schoolgirl, gladdened that her suitor was in robust health.

Though it was early, Owen called in to Prospect's saloon. The bar was practically a round-the-clock business. Owen would not permit excessive drunkenness in his town. However, the saloon was always open to travellers who had ridden all night, or men knocking off after a night shift. There were indeed a few drinkers there already. They looked weary as they sipped their beers. Owen was not tempted to join them. He was looking for information.

The bar was tended by the saloon's proprietor, Lee Charles. Even when Owen had been a boy, Lee had seemed very old. With his long white hair and beard, and patient manner, he was not unlike a druid. He naturally heard all the rumours from the drinkers coming and going. Owen was interested to learn what Lee knew about the shadowy figure whom he had clashed with.

Lee had not always been a bartender and family man. Though Owen could not remember anybody else behind the bar of the saloon, Lee was a relative newcomer to Prospect. In his early twenties, Lee had been a prospector in South Dakota.

Like so many other settlers to the Americas, he had been raised on his parents' dairy farm. Lee had been contented enough; the output of the Charles' farm was sufficient, though they were far from wealthy. Lee knew the drills very well, and enjoyed the routine and the predictability. The dawn woke Lee and his parents. It was a demanding, arduous day, but it made Lee hardened and strong. As the night drew in, Lee would return to the family's small house. He would typically drop into deep sleep, his pleasant exhaustion driving him into a satisfied slumber.

Lee dreamt of nothing more than the familiar simplicity of the farm, until the day at the drugstore when he encountered Lucas Evans. Lucas, like him, was a farmer's son from a neighbouring farm. It was only rarely that Lee ventured into town for supplies, and he was only on nodding terms with Lucas. While Lee was normally easygoing with no spectacular ambitions, Lucas was pushy and persuasive. Chatting at the store, Lucas had described the gold rush in South Dakota. There was a mountain range in Indian country that was riddled with the precious metal. Hundreds of men had travelled there and sifted through the muddy river waters, and found riches.

'Sure, it's dirty, dangerous work,' the teenage Lucas had extolled knowingly. 'But when you hit that big find – well, you've made it, Lee.' Lee had laughed the tale off. He could not picture himself leaving his farm behind to chance it searching for gold in the hills.

Yet, not two weeks later, Lee found himself reluctantly sitting opposite Lucas in the back of a covered wagon. Lucas was not yet old enough to purchase liquor in a saloon, yet he spoke with confidence and imagined life experience. Lucas had planted a seed in the minds of his own parents; the Charles family had soon found themselves in conference with the Evans family. The conclusion of this powwow was that Lucas and Lee would make fine partners in a gold prospecting mission.

They shared the cramped wagon with a dozen other would-be gold millionaires. Lucas had been zealous and excitable. He had led the little gold crew in songs and travelling games. Though Lee had smiled politely, he was not certain that this little adventure was in fact occurring. Over the weeks it took to reach Redforest, the ugly reality of the situation began to weigh on Lee.

He had learned something else about Lucas as well. Though Lucas had benefited from a similar upbringing to him, he had somehow turned out to be a spoiled loud mouth. The gold crew were tiring of the nonsense he spoke and his ridiculous, empty boasts. Lee predicted that Lucas would be bad news.

Lee recalled vividly the first day of prospecting at

Redforest. He and Lucas had risen early. The dawn sky was a charcoal, sodden grey. A thick mist hovered over the hills, and the prospectors had to fight their way through it. When the two had arrived at their chosen spot at the riverside, Lee had resigned himself to his fate. Lucas was as energetic as ever – at least, at first.

Crouched beside the river in the frigid cold, Lucas and Lee had sieved through the mud. Though Lee resented his predicament, he had never feared a hard day's work. He grudgingly soldiered on. Lucas struggled with the patience and solid graft necessary. The truth of prospecting for gold was not as pretty as Lucas imagined. Lucas would grind for an hour or two, throw his sieve down, and then waste a lot of time bothering the other prospectors.

With Lee's determined approach, he was naturally the first to find a sprinkling of gold dust in his sieve. Lee hoped to keep his find quiet: it was hardly big money. Lucas, though, could not contain his excitement. The two dairy farmers' sons had a loose agreement that they were partners and would split their finds. Though Lucas was clearly a lot lazier than Lee, Lee did not want a fuss. Lee was angry, though, that the whole of Redforest suddenly knew about the find.

Cleansing his sieve, Lee put the tiny pebbles of gold in his wallet, folded in a sheet of paper. He had heard of fool's gold, and was not going to start spending until he was sure. Lucas was not as prudent. As the whole town knew of their find, it was easy for Lucas to enjoy credit at the saloons and gambling dens. Redforest was a lawless township. The sheriff was a lawman in name only: he in fact had his fingers in many rotten pies.

Lee was forced to confront Lucas. He was laid-back and patient by nature, but he had to give Lucas a mouthful.

'You gotta pull yourself together, Lucas! We ain't sold this gold yet. We don't even know what it's worth. Let's get back to the riverside and get on with our work.'

Lucas had angrily shoved Lee away like a petulant baby, and wandered off to make more trouble.

The patience of the bartenders and croupiers did not last long. Lucas had disappeared for a few days. Lee did not see him again until he heard badly disguised tiptoes in their shared boarding room. Lee slept with his wallet for safety, and sure enough, he awoke to find Lucas reaching under his blanket.

Furious, Lee grasped Lucas's wrist and sprang from his bed. Lucas was armed: he pointed his six-shooter directly at Lucas's forehead.

'You give it to me, Lee. It's mine and you know it.'

Lee surrendered. He reached into his pocket and handed over his wallet.

Lee learned something new about himself that day, an aspect of his character he had never known before. He was a killer.

As Lucas had fled from the filthy little room like a startled rodent, Lee had reached for his rifle. He had until tonight only used it for hunting. As his former business partner – if you could call him that – had sprinted into the night, Lee had accurately landed a single bullet in the back of Lucas's head. Lucas dropped to the muddy ground of Redforest's main street, and Lee recalled feeling nothing but contempt.

Lee had feared the jailhouse or even the noose in the

aftermath but he was taken aback by how he was viewed. The townsfolk (including the sheriff) had expressed their thanks for ridding Redforest of such a troublesome rodent. They made sure the gold was safely returned to him. Lee could feel people looking at him in a different light.

Prospecting was a filthy business. To find the riches, if ever you could, took weeks or months of limbs blackened by sticky mud in the freezing cold. Yet, as Lee dwelt on his killing of Lucas, he began to feel that his soul was equally dirtied. Lee's tenacity – and perhaps the unwillingness of anyone to distract him – led to a few more lucky finds. With his booty safely hidden away, Lee suddenly left Redforest without saying goodbye. Lee traded the gold for dollars. Seeking a new life as far from Redforest as he could, Lee chanced it in Prospect. Starting out as a barkeeper, Lee had later bought the saloon from the retiring owner. In the meantime, he had started a family.

Nobody knew of Lee's wicked secret. Lee was resolved to keep it that way.

The sheriff burst through the batwing doors. Lee nodded to acknowledge the sheriff's arrival. The bartender was highly industrious, and as sprightly as a much younger man. Of course, Lee had by now heard his customers' empty speculation regarding Renard's disappearance. Renard had been abducted by redskins, or he'd run away with a child bride, or possibly even retired in secret to a monastery. While Lee was amused to hear the baseless stories, he never opined himself. He was wise, and only commented on matters of fact.

'Good morning to you, Lee. I could use your input on

something.' Lee took Owen over to a quiet table. It was not busy, and Lee could leave the bar unattended for a short while.

The sheriff summarized the chain of events. Lee was aghast, but maintained his cool exterior. The barkeeper had always had the utmost respect for the sheriff. It was shocking to learn that he had become a target for an unknown killer. All this tittle-tattle in the bar, he mused. The truth was crazier. Owen concluded his outline of his ordeal.

'Can you help me, Lee? Have you heard anything about this character in black?'

Lee paused, pondering the whole situation. The barman was a businessman and also a family man. Though he had lost his wife some time ago, his adult children and his grandchildren lived in Prospect. Lee was friendly and approachable, but ultimately a very serious individual. He had a notion that the sheriff was stuck.

'Sheriff, I got to admit I'm surprised by your request. That's some crazy story. I hear all kinda talk here in the saloon. I never indulge myself in spreading any dumb stories, though. What I can do, though, is repeat some of the crazy talk I've heard. You can be the judge.'

'Please, Lee. Go on.'

'Had a dude in here once, a young feller. Too much drink in him. He was some kinda thief. Plain stupid to boast about his thieving for everyone to hear. He kept referrin' to a man behind the scenes, though. Said that nobody knew his name, not everyone had seen him. Gave orders through middlemen.'

Owen could tell that Lee was reviewing this rumour in

his mind. It did not seem such a tall story, now.

'Now this young guy, he called this mystery man the Boss Man. He was all "the Boss Man's gonna like this, I'm gonna show this to the Boss Man." Now this kid was with a crowd of other young boys. This little gang tried to carry out a bank robbery in El Paso – they all got shot. Stupid kids.

'Never paid this story any real mind, but now I wonder who this Boss Man is. People mention him now and again, like the boogieman. Just thought it was a fancy story. But something else makes me think. This Boss Man runs an outlaw gang. People talk about them like they're devils or something. These outlaws – they murder, rob, hold up stagecoaches. They call themselves the Blood Masks – on account of the red scarves they tie round their faces.'

Owen felt an icy frisson in his bones.

'Sheriff, all I'm doin' is repeating saloon talk. The Blood Masks? The Boss Man? It's probably all bull. We've never seen these so-called Blood Masks here in Prospect. The Boss Man calling the shots from the shadows? Hell, any crook would do that. All I'm saying is that your run-ins reminded me of these stories.'

Owen thanked Lee, who returned to tending the bar. The sheriff sat a while at the table. He stroked his chin thoughtfully. Crazy stories such as this reached his ear from time to time, but Owen paid them no mind. There were striking similarities between this rumour, though, and Owen's own experiences. Both the stranger at Renard's house and Owen's would-be killer had carried red kerchiefs. Could the assassin in black be one and the same as this Boss Man? And how did Renard fit into it all?

The cool dawn had passed now, and the air in the saloon had grown stifling. Owen could tell that it would be another day of fiery heat. While his morning cheer had now faded, none of his resolve had. The information from Lee was a slim clue – but there was something in it. Owen would have to probe further.

Just as Owen stood up to leave the saloon, one of the drinkers approached him. He had been sat in the shade with his hat protecting his face, but now Owen recognized him.

Mordecai.

CHAPTER 18

'Couldn't help overhearing, Sheriff. The Blood Masks, huh? Think I heard a thing or two about them.'

Mordecai sat himself down opposite Owen. He had carried over his bottle of beer with him, and took a sip. Owen sat back down.

'How can you help me, sir?' entreated Owen.

Mordecai took another sip.

'Since your visit yesterday, I been thinking a lot about this Arthur character. About this stranger showing up dead at the schoolteacher's house. Now I don't know if it was Arthur, but that boy sure was crazy.'

Pausing to draw from the bottle again, Mordecai's eyes saddened. 'The men at Saint Jude – well, some might say they're lost souls. Nowhere to go, nothing to lose, so they end up at the mine. I'm kinda in charge there – not that we hold committee meetings or such like. I'm like a father to those men.'

To Owen, this seemed to be an oddly personal touch to Mordecai's description. The miner had struck Owen as a granite-faced character, and he wondered how many beers Mordecai had drunk.

'Yeah, we get nutcases and wild boys, but we're good at straightening them out. But Arthur. . . .' Mordecai's voice seemed to break, and he quickly took another gulp of beer. Owen remained silent. The miner seemed to want to get something off his chest.

'Well, I just feel bad for the boy, Sheriff. He was hard-working and smart. Dunno what he was doing at Saint Jude to begin with – 'cept he was just so crazy. He feels like a failure to me. Maybe I could've helped him. '

'Mordecai, did Arthur ever speak of the Blood Masks?'

'He sure did, Sheriff. A heck of a lot. But he was always telling tall tales. I never believed none of it. He said many a time that he rode with the Blood Masks. He told it like some campfire tale. That he belonged to these outlaws with red masks, that they had a mysterious leader no one had ever seen. Hell, he also said he'd been on an expedition to hunt Aztec gold. I tell you, this Arthur had had some schooling. You can't invent stories like that without reading a few books.'

Mordecai was getting worked up now, and took a noisy slurp on the beer bottle.

'But these Blood Masks – they were Arthur's favourite story. The way he described them was so far-fetched, but so detailed. To begin with, the men liked hearing the story. But then he went on and on and on about them, and we soon tired of it. There was one particular Blood Masks story which stuck in my memory.

'According to Arthur, they were all blood brothers. They carried out some kind of ceremony like the Red Indians do. The outlaws had spies and gunmen all over the country, waiting in secret. They were nomadic, but they also had a main base. Apparently, they lived together in a cave in the hills. The Blood Masks only carried out a robbery after lots of watching, and they did it quickly and professionally. They weren't afraid to kill, but they just didn't like no mess.

'Now Arthur told us about a holdup they done in the town of Chastity. First of all, they had a spy on the staff of the bank. He worked there for months, maybe even years, gaining the trust of the manager and the customers. Now – being a Blood Mask – this employee was also an expert pickpocket. He slipped the keys for the vault away from the manager, and – Lord knows how – they copied them. Then, the spy returned the keys to the manager. All of this without the manager suspecting a thing, of course!'

Mordecai smiled at the preposterous story, and continued.

'So, one night, the Blood Masks had a clear run at the bank. They disguised their faces with those red scarves, then rode into town late at night. With the keys, there was nothing to stop them. They opened up without a single gunshot, but they didn't have the combination for the safe. Now this is where this boy Arthur came in. He was the dynamite man. In the middle of the night, right in the middle of Chastity, Arthur blew up the safe. 'Course, the explosion attracted a lot of attention. But the Blood Masks were fast. Quick as lightning, they collected all the cash and jewellery – which must have been blown all over the place. Then they disappeared into the night.'

Mordecai winked knowingly at the end of the story. His grin faded when he began discussing Arthur again.

'Thing is, Sheriff, this Arthur really did seem to know

about dynamite and such. Like I said at the mine, he was so crazy that I never let him near no explosives. But it was like he knew what he was talking about. Like maybe he really had used explosives, some.'

As outrageous as the Blood Masks stories were, Owen felt that he was on to something. Not so long ago, Owen would have paid these tales no mind. Now, though, the Blood Masks appeared to be showing up everywhere he looked.

'Mordecai, I've been hearing a lot about these apparent Blood Masks lately. I'm going to look into a link between the gang and Arthur. Can you tell me any hard facts – who they are, where they are based?'

'Arthur always said their hideout was in the hills outside Chastity. Chastity ain't too far away. You could try asking around there. That's if you're seriously looking into this thing, Sheriff. I never thought too much about Arthur's tall tales.'

Thanking Mordecai, Owen stood up to leave, but the miner had a question for the lawman.

'Sheriff, just one thing. Will you let me know what became of Arthur – send word to Saint Jude? I can't help thinking about the boy.'

'I will, Mordecai.'

'And one more thing, Sheriff. Watch your back.'

CHAPTER 19

The ride to Chastity seemed to pass rapidly for Owen. His journeys to Saint Jude and Blackwood had felt like ordeals, but the new information the sheriff had learned had filled his mind with ideas. While the clues were only tentative, Owen felt certain he was on to something. The notion that the Blood Masks were real, and had him in their crosshairs, was unnerving. However, Owen's friend was still absent. The sheriff was not willing to yield to this mysterious gang's scare tactics.

He had dozens of questions for the sheriff of Chastity. Owen had worked with Chastity's head law enforcer on occasion. The town of Chastity had been founded by German settlers, and the language was still widely spoken there. The local sheriff, Dieter Hanover, was himself of German stock. Though he was American by birth and spoke English as his first language, Dieter retained more than a touch of European reserve and stoicism.

Owen had collaborated with Dieter during a case of cattle theft. It was Owen's first encounter with the Chastity lawman. Owen had suspected that animals stolen from Prospect were being funnelled through Chastity, and possibly even sold there. He had been reluctant to draw another lawman into the affair. Dieter had trouble enough in his own town, Owen thought. He did not need to do another settlement's police work as well. Dieter, though, was very cooperative – in his own, highly detached way.

On that first occasion, Owen had ridden into Chastity and called at Dieter's office. The sheriff did not exactly welcome Owen warmly. Dieter was not so much a man of few words, as an economic and efficient speaker. He spoke when he had something to say, and did not embellish his words with exaggeration nor emotion. Owen had, at first, found Dieter's calculated silences and sparse words disconcerting.

'Sit down, Sheriff Rowlands,' Dieter had commanded. His words had come across as more of an instruction than an invitation. 'Explain to me your problem.'

Owen had related the incidences of theft and his reason for believing a link to Chastity. During Owen's explanation, Dieter had listened in grave silence. Dieter boasted a shock of dirty blonde curls, and hypnotic blue eyes. So hushed was Dieter that Owen thought he had stopped listening. Finally, Dieter had broken the silence.

'Very well, Sheriff Rowlands. I will help you. Please follow me out of Chastity. I have an idea where these thieves could be.'

Owen had followed Dieter as the two had ridden out of Chastity. Dieter was unspeaking as he led the way. Owen was uncertain what to make of his character. He seemed to be supremely confident, yet his taciturn manner was worrying. Owen was not certain where

Dieter was taking them, nor what he was planning.

Their pace had slowed when they approached a camp on the plains. Three of the missing cows were tied up there, and Owen recognized his two suspects. They were busying themselves setting up a campfire.

'I noticed these two characters passing through Chastity, Sheriff Rowlands. I did not like the look of them, so I kept an eye on them. I will help you apprehend them.'

The two lawmen drew their weapons and approached the camp. Owen would ask the thieves to surrender, but he was expecting a fight. Theft of cattle was a hanging offence.

'Hello, the camp,' Owen called out to them.

When the rustlers saw the two armed sheriffs, they knew they had been rumbled. Owen saw one of the thieves motioning for his own Colt, but Owen was too fast. He fired his revolver and eliminated the thief with a well-aimed shot. The rustler collapsed to his knees, and lurched forward, a single drop of blood on his chest.

Instinctively, Owen clicked the revolver to turn the cylinder for another shot. He knew that the thief's accomplice would be just as belligerent. The single second while Owen readied his gun was almost fatal for him, though. It gave the second thief time to aim a shot and fire.

Dieter, though, was too fast. He almost psychically knew the thief's movements, and Dieter brutally fired before the rustler could respond. The second thief had been shot down.

For a few moments, the only sounds were the fading reports of the weapons and the indifferent moos of the cows. Owen felt ramrod stiff, but Dieter was unfazed.

'Sheriff Rowlands, let us return to Chastity. We will make arrangements for the cows and the dead men to be recovered.'

While Dieter could easily be viewed as a reptilian killer, Owen believed that he had developed an affinity for the man. Dieter had put himself in danger for a visiting lawman, and Dieter's quick-thinking may well have saved Owen's life. Despite his outward coldness, Dieter was a brave and dedicated officer of the peace. In the following years, Owen and Dieter had worked together a number of times. They had not exactly developed a friendship – Dieter was too icy and remote. Owen believed, though, that he had found a loyal ally.

Owen was looking forward to any input Dieter had into the affair of Renard and the Blood Masks.

Riding into Chastity, the sheriff was glad to see the familiar surroundings. It was a busy morning, and the air was dusty from the comings and goings. With somebody like Dieter in charge, Chastity was peaceful and prosperous and Owen felt safe riding the dirty streets.

The sheriff eagerly rode directly to Dieter's office. He tied his roan to the rails and knocked politely on the door. If Dieter was glad to see Owen, he did not reveal it. Dieter's face was as granite as always.

'Sheriff Rowlands,' he greeted. Even after several years, Dieter always addressed Owen as Sheriff. 'I was about to contact you. I think you will be very interested to see who I have locked up in the jailhouse.'

CHAPTER 20

Dieter was uncharacteristically loquacious in describing how Karl came to be locked up in the cells in the sheriff's office.

'I noticed him sneaking into town last night. He had obviously waited until after dark. I saw him through the window of my office.' Dieter was born and raised in Chastity, yet still spoke in crisp, almost accentless tones. Owen was reminded of a narrator in a stage play.

The sheriff could easily imagine Dieter keeping a midnight vigil. He was like a clockwork man, designed purely for law enforcement. Owen seriously doubted that Dieter went home every evening and cuddled his wife. Not that Dieter had ever discussed any kind of private life.

'I didn't like what I saw. The man had obviously been badly beaten up. When I arrested him, the man refused to speak. I wondered if you knew anything about him.'

Dieter did not elaborate on his encounter with Owen's would-be murderer. Owen knew well, though, that he would have fought ferociously. Dieter humbly brushed over how he overcame the killer. Owen's fellow sheriff did not exhibit any scratches, nor welts.

Owen was glad to share his experiences with Dieter. The Chastity lawman listened intently. If he was shocked or concerned, his features revealed nothing.

'I am happy to leave him in your custody, Sheriff Rowlands. However, might I share an idea with you?'

'I'd be glad to hear it, Dieter.'

'Sheriff Rowlands, here in Chastity, the Blood Masks are more than just a campfire tale. They have been sighted several times, but I have never caught them in the act. Serious crimes are not common in Chastity.'

Owen admired this touch of modesty. Dieter was feared and respected. He watched over Chastity like a vengeful angel. Few criminals would dare to do something to attract his pitiless attentions.

'There was a stage coach robbery two weeks ago. Two men on horseback – both wearing red masks – held up the coach. The passengers were a very wealthy family. The thieves took all their jewellery and cash. The passengers were a husband and wife, and their two children. They were not hurt. The thieves were armed with rifles, though. From the descriptions of the attack, they sounded experienced and professional. The situation could have been a lot worse.

'Unfortunately, I could not hunt down the robbers. I took some deputies, and we searched up and down the road and the surrounding land. We found nothing.'

Dieter paused for a second. Though his face betrayed no emotion, Owen thought he could detect a note of frustration in his voice.

'I think the Blood Masks knew who was on that coach. You have heard the stories. They have spies everywhere. I have heard many reports of this gang being seen in this area. There are too many sightings for them to be wishful thinking. I believe that the Blood Masks have a hiding place in this area.'

On hearing this, Owen leaned forward in his seat, his lawman's antennae prickling. He was getting closer.

'You could be right, Dieter, but that stranger in your cell ain't gonna talk.'

'Sheriff Rowlands, you know I'm not much of a talker.' The two lawmen paced cautiously to the cells behind Dieter's office. Owen would lead the interrogation. The building boasted three jail cells, but only one was occupied today. Approaching the prisoner, Owen felt a current of anger surge through him. He was grateful that Dieter was there to restrain him, should he become carried away by his fury.

Karl lay back on the simple pew in the cell. His night in the wilds, following a brutal thrashing by Owen, and then Dieter's merciless arrest, had sapped him. He was actually a little glad for a day's rest. Karl would escape from this particular jam. He always won in the end.

Despite his fatigue, Karl arrogantly perked up when Dieter unlocked the cell door. He would enjoy taunting the two sheriffs. Vain as he was, he did not think the two lawmen were idiots. He in fact enjoyed the challenge of riling them up.

Owen began.

'Stranger, I'm going to ask you again. What is your name?'

'What does it matter, Sheriff? You got me. I'm gonna

hang if you know my name or not.'

'The more you cooperate, the easier the judge will be on you.' Owen had to spit his next words out. 'If you help us, I'll put in a good word for you.'

Karl laughed caustically. He continued to bray mockingly when Owen raised his fist. He was blocked by Dieter, though. He silently sprang between Owen and Karl. Dieter's cautionary glare at Owen made words unnecessary. Owen took a pace backwards.

'OK then, stranger. We found the red scarf on you. What can you tell us about the Blood Masks? I know you're part of a gang.'

Karl looked upward to the ceiling in pretend boredom.

'Please, Sheriff. You've asked me all this before. The Blood Masks? Honestly, Sheriff! Do you believe in fairies?'

Owen's grilling went on for some time. Karl did not tire of insulting the sheriffs, or giving meaningless, defiant answers. Several times, Dieter had to lay his hand gently on Owen's shoulder to remind him to keep his composure. At the end of the encounter, the sheriffs seemed to have grown weary before Karl did.

With a sigh, Owen addressed Dieter.

'Come on, Sheriff Hanover. Let's try again tomorrow. This low-life ain't going anywhere.'

Owen slammed the cell door behind him. The two lawmen returned to Dieter's office.

'Dieter, this boy is not gonna spill the beans. I've got to admit, he's testing my patience.'

Owen nodded towards the cell keys, dangling by an iron bangle from Dieter's waist. Dieter felt the keys and nodded back, knowingly. The stranger had, somehow, removed the key to his cell from Dieter's belt.

Owen smiled.

CHAPTER 21

For the first time since his investigations began, Owen felt pure excitement. While he was still perplexed and troubled by Renard's disappearance, he had taken a positive step forward. The strange assassin was clearly linked to the mystery. Allowing him to take the keys was a very clever idea by Dieter. Owen knew, though, that the killer was as devious as a rat. Whether the outlaw was on to their ruse or not, he would be watching for pursuers when he fled the jail cell.

As night fell, Owen had positioned himself behind the drugstore building adjacent to Dieter's office. He had had time to rest and eat during the day. Dieter had gone about his sheriff's rounds as usual, but never straying too far from the jailhouse. Throughout the day, Karl had remained in his cell, cocky as always. The two lawmen knew that the killer might dart at any moment, but that an escape after dark was more likely.

Chastity was illuminated by the stars and the moon. The ethereal, silver light seemed to add to Owen's agitation. From his hiding place, he observed a light on in Dieter's office. He knew that before long, Dieter would extinguish his lamp and pretend to leave for the night. As the sheriff's window fell into pure darkness, Dieter walked out of the building. He had left his horse in the corral behind the office. Joining Owen in his hiding place, the two silently kept watch. Despite his pretence of indifference, the lawmen knew that their quarry was daring and slippery. He would not be able to resist an opportunity to escape.

Though Dieter maintained his quiet intensity, Owen was restless. He was hungry to learn where the outlaw would lead them. Their vigil seemed endless, yet there was no relief when they saw the shadowy figure emerge from the jail cells. As predicted, the stranger went around the back of the office to the corral. They heard the horses stir, and then the sounds of galloping. It appeared that the killer was riding back towards the rocky hills.

Owen was about to pursue, when Dieter stopped him.

'Not yet, Sheriff Rowlands. Give him some time. He will know if he is being followed. We will take the utmost care.'

Dieter made them wait nearly half an hour. Owen was growing frantic, but Dieter calmly reassured him. As they set off after the assassin, Dieter took the lead. He said that he could hear the outlaw's stolen horse in the distance, and even in the dark he could keep an eye out for tracks. Owen's patience was further tried when Dieter insisted that they trotted along at a cautious pace. Dieter was mindful of alerting their quarry.

As agitated as he was, Owen admitted to himself that he would have struggled to follow the trail without Dieter. A wolf expertly hunting its prey, Dieter even seemed to be able to see in the darkness. Owen was trusting his companion completely. The hills were labyrinthine by night, and but for the moonlight, the pair would have been navigating blindly. Dieter instinctively knew how to find passage, though.

Owen had grown up not far from the rocky mountain. As a child, he had played in the hills. His boyish games, though, had only given him a limited knowledge of the terrain. As the two lawmen explored the stony paths, Owen remarked what an effective hiding place the hills could be. Away from meddling eyes, with thousands of nooks to slip into, and a powerful view overlooking Prospect, Chastity and Blackwood.

Dwelling on this, Owen also wondered what character of men would choose to live here. Surely, only savages, or the truly desperate, would roost in this granite nest. Owen's attacker, though, was of this nature. Here in this rocky hideaway, he would be welcomed as kin by the tarantulas and the scorpions.

Dieter suddenly pulled on his reins.

'Can you hear that, Sheriff Rowlands?'

'No, Dieter.'

Owen wondered what Dieter had sensed. Dieter dismounted gingerly, and Owen followed. They were climbing a steep path, which reached a long plateau above them. On foot, the two stealthily approached the flat ground. During the ride, Owen's eyes had adapted to the inky shadows. On the plateau, Owen could make out shady movements, and pinpricks of light from torches and lanterns. There was a camp of some sort on the ridge. Owen estimated that there were perhaps a dozen men there. He could hear subdued chatter. Some of the men had bedded down for the night, whilst others were busying themselves. Owen thought he could see several horses there as well.

Dieter urged Owen to lie down prone to avoid detection. They each reached for their Colts, but did not cock the weapons. It seemed that they had discovered the stranger's outlaw gang. They did not know whether these men were the so-called Blood Masks.

Dieter and Owen had little chance of overpowering the gang, whoever they were. From past experiences, Owen knew that Dieter was bold, but also very calculating. He would not stupidly confront a dozen men in the dark. They had succeeded in finding the lair of the band of brigands. Perhaps they should return with men of their own, or at least wait until daylight.

The click of a gun being cocked startled the lawmen.

They turned to find Karl standing over them, his own Colt drawn. Even in the darkness, the sheriffs could see the beam of his arrogant smile. Under the glimmer of the stars, half of his face in shadow, the killer truly looked maniacally evil.'Good evening, Sheriffs,' he guffawed mockingly. 'You know, you really had me. I honest to God thought I'd gotten away from you. Got to hand it to you – you boys can follow a trail.'

He lit a cheap cigar with his free hand.

' 'Bout time I introduced myself properly. My name's Karl. Some people call me the Boss Man of the Blood Masks. I'm happy to share my little secret with you, 'cause in a little while, I'm gonna kill you both.'

CHAPTER 22

'Drop your weapons,' Karl commanded. The sheriffs unenthusiastically obeyed.

Facing their foe, with their backs to the camp, the law officers nevertheless detected the approach of somebody behind them. Owen and Dieter stiffly and fearfully turned their necks to peer, but Karl stopped them masterfully.

'Keep your eyes on me. My men also have their weapons drawn on your backs. You ain't going nowhere. 'Cept hell.'

Owen's thoughts raced. He was flustered and angered by the situation. Dieter displayed his usual outward calm, but Owen did not doubt that he, too, was panicking. One question which struck Owen was why Karl did not make an immediate execution. He wondered what the murderer was contemplating.

'Now I'm going to march you up to my camp. So turn slowly.'

They did. Dieter and Owen rotated their bodies cautiously, to find two gunmen with their Colts readied. While Karl was a lean and striking figure, his servants did not resemble him in any way. One was short, dumpy and double-chinned. He grinned childishly, clearly pleased that he had the upper hand. The other gunman was also diminutive, yet wiry and slight. Were it not for his wizened face and greying hair, he could have passed for a schoolboy.

His first thought was that these two bandits were weaklings. They were clearly drawn to Karl by his commanding presence. The two crooks – as dangerous as they clearly were – were not unlike the cronies of a school bully.

The two gunmen were not wearing their red bandanas. That they were willing to reveal their faces was a fact that bothered Owen.

He felt a sharp and cruel kick to his lower back, which caused the two gunmen to snigger idiotically.

'Move!' Karl commanded.

The two sheriffs slowly paced up the incline to the flat ridge. As they passed the undersized crooks, they noticed the camp stirring. They trudged towards the base, guided by spiteful pokes in the back from Karl's revolver. Owen felt his bile rising. He wanted to tear Karl's flesh away, inch by agonizing inch.

In the middle of the camp, the dozen men had gathered around in a circle for a good look at their new toys. A few even prodded the sheriffs with sticks, giggling like little girls.

Karl took charge of the situation. He spoke as if he was a General making a speech to his troops.

'Welcome to our fortress in the hills, Sheriffs. We been hiding out here for a few years, now. Raiding towns all over the territory. Looks mighty poor, don't it? No

112

saloon, no ablutions, no women. Well, we got plenty of cash stashed away. And none of you lawmen have caught us!'

Karl's repost caused a murmur of sycophantic laughter amongst his soldiers. The outlaw leader approached Owen, deliberately standing uncomfortably close to him. Karl's face was less than an inch from Owen's, close enough for Owen to smell his cheap cigar smoke. The killer's demeanour changed. He became serious and sullen, speaking in artificial, menacing whispers.

'What do you say, Sheriff? I'd say we had a score to settle.' It seemed to Owen that, despite Karl's conceited exterior, there was a little part of him that was unnerved that he had been bested by both Owen and Dieter.

Seeing the so-called Blood Masks at close quarters, and what a rabble they were, emboldened Owen. Karl's cowardly threat filled Owen with contempt, and he could hold his tongue no longer.

'I can't tell you how disappointed I am, Karl. We heard all these dumb stories about the Blood Masks and you are just . . . dumb.' Owen noticed Karl trying to conceal an angry tremble in his jowls, but this only invigorated him. 'A bunch of kids in Hallowe'en masks.'

Karl struck Owen in his gut with a powerful swing of his fist. The Blood Masks cheered ingratiatingly. Owen groaned as he doubled over in pain. He could tell, though, that his caustic words had burned Karl's pride and that Karl styled himself as some sort of master criminal. It would not do for him to be belittled in front of his men.

Karl began striding back and forth, like a college professor pacing the podium as he gave a lecture. Owen's taunt had unsettled him. Except for a handful of highly able men, his gang were indeed a gaggle. However, the sheriff still had much to learn about his criminal army. Once again, the General addressed his troops.

'Well, well, boys. Sheriff Rowlands is too smart for us. And his little buddy here ain't saying nothing!' Karl offensively cupped Dieter's chin in his hand and gave it a little shake. 'I'd say we had a couple more surprises lined up for our unexpected guests. Wouldn't you agree, boys?'

The Blood Masks again cheered, although the sheriffs had the sense that the robbers did not understand what Karl was talking about.

'Why don't we introduce the sheriffs to our other guest, huh?'

There was another roar of agreement from the crowd. Without prompting, two of the outlaws forcibly jostled Dieter and Owen along with prods from their six-shooters. Karl strode over to a cave at the far side of the plateau. The Blood Masks forced the lawmen to follow. Karl was carrying a lantern, and gestured for the sheriffs to enter the opening in the hillside.

'Enjoy your stay, boys. Don't try nothing. We'll be watching all night. I'm sure the three of you will get on just fine.' Karl handed the lantern to one of his lackeys, and shoved each of the lawmen into the cave.

The outlaw keeping guard deliberately shone the lantern into the cave. He was doing more than watching over his charges. This whole stunt was obviously part of Karl's plan. Though the darkness within the hole was impenetrable, the light was sufficient to reveal a pathetic shape cowering in a corner. He looked up when Dieter and Owen were bundled into the opening. Though the figure was dressed in rags, and had obviously received a beating, Owen recognized him instantly.

Renard.

CHAPTER 23

Renard tried to hide behind trembling hands when Owen rushed over to him. It was upsetting to Owen to see his old friend shying away so pathetically. Renard had always been so erudite and distinguished. Now, though, he had been reduced to a frightened mess. The old man recoiled when Owen attempted to comfort him with a hand upon his shoulder.

'Renard, it's so good to see you. My partner here is Sheriff Dieter Hanover – he's the sheriff of Chastity. I don't know what the heck happened to you, Renard, but we will get you out of this hole.'

Renard peeped through his fingers, as his hands nervously protected his face.

'Owen? Owen Rowlands?' The sight of his old friend lifted Renard's feelings, despite the deadly circumstances. 'Dear God! I'm so glad you're here!' The two old friends embraced, ignoring the pains they had both suffered.

Though Dieter said nothing, he too was pleased to see the reunion. It had only been four days since Renard had vanished. Dieter could only conjecture at what miseries the retired schoolteacher had endured.

'Are you all right, Renard? Looks like you took a real hiding,' Owen said.

Renard's retort was surprisingly upbeat, and he could not help smiling.

'I could make the same comment of you, Owen! Lord knows what you've been through.'

Renard sighed. He did not need to be prompted. His guests were longing to learn what had become of him. Even though the watchmen were still listening outside, Renard began.

'Like you, I'd heard about these Blood Masks. As you know, I am something of an amateur scholar with Greek myths and European legends. I enjoy a good yarn, even if it is fantastical. At the saloon or chatting at the drug-store, a couple of people had related tales of this criminal enterprise. I was amused to hear the stories, but I paid them no mind. They were far-fetched – and we had most surely never seen these legendary outlaws in Prospect.'

Renard was gaining some composure, which gave a little encouragement and reassurance to Dieter and Owen. It was gladdening to hear his articulate, eloquent words once again. Whatever had befallen him, he was in one physical piece.

'That was until Friday evening. I was at leisure in my house, enjoying a brandy and my pipe. Sat in my parlour, I had a book on my lap when there was a pounding at the door. Not a polite knocking, you see, but somebody forcing their way in. The door burst open and a small group of young men entered. Each had veiled his fea-tures with a scarlet neckerchief. The Blood Masks, as I

117

was soon to learn.

'No, I did not stop to chat. I rose to confront them, but they pushed me back in my seat. They ransacked my house. I knew not what they searched for. Valuables, I suppose, but I keep few of them in my home. Struggling, I like to think I gave a good account of myself – even at my age. They were too many, and too strong, though. With one of these ne'er do wells – something of a wretch, to my own mind – I struck a fortunate blow. I believe I may have rendered him unconscious.

'The whole encounter lasted not longer than a few moments – although to me it seemed a lot longer. They bundled a sack over my head and made off to the hills.

'They are unlike other outlaws, these Blood Masks. I do not know their master plan, exactly, but they clearly sought more than the family jewellery. They seek to keep me alive – for some nefarious reason I know not. I have no family to pay a ransom.'

While Aunty Jasmine would have lacked the cash to pay blood money, Owen did not add that Renard did in fact have a living relative.

'But now, my boys, how will we escape these fiends?'

Renard looked outside at the watchman. He clearly caught the guard's eye. Renard had never lacked pluck. The watchman shone his lantern directly in Renard's eye, and cocked his weapon with his free hand.

Owen and Dieter had listened carefully. Though they could not hear each other's thoughts, the two had in fact arrived at similar analyses.

Firstly, Renard was on to something when he referred to this 'nefarious reason'. The Blood Masks were keeping him alive, when they had had opportunity to rob him and leave him for dead. Perhaps they knew more about him than they were revealing. It had become clear to Owen that Renard hid a number of secrets.

Moreover, though the Blood Masks had also threatened to kill Dieter and Owen, they had not. What did that signify? It was possible that revealing Renard to the two men was merely an act of mockery. Nevertheless, Dieter and Owen were unarmed. It would only take a few seconds to shoot them dead, but the Blood Masks had left them largely unharmed.

Secondly, the lawmen had read something in Renard's words. Owen had never found Renard to be boastful. While he loved myths and legends, he never propounded tall tales of his own. Renard's description of knocking Arthur unconscious was only part of the story. Arthur had received a vicious thrashing that had killed him. Renard had also omitted any mention of Jasmine. His aunty was plainly a drunken embarrassment, but Owen's friend was not being candid.

As officers of the law, Dieter and Owen had enjoyed sufficient experience of dishonesty to be able to tell.

Renard was lying.

Listening from the shadows, Karl made his own analysis of Renard's account. Karl, too, concluded that it was all lies.

CHAPTER 24

The three captives had not slept. Owen and Dieter had not confronted Renard's lies during the night. They had tried to console him, the three lying next to each other for warmth. Though the prisoners had huddled in sleepless silence, their guard had been less careful. The watchman had sat on a rock throughout the night. When he had tired of holding up his lantern and Navy Colt, he had put the weapon away and lain the lamp on the ground. The guard had obviously tried to stay awake, but ultimately his body had surrendered to slumber. Nobody had come to relieve him.

As the sun rose, the light gave Dieter and Owen a good view of the snoozing lookout. From the cave, they did not have a strong view of the Blood Masks' base. However, it was still early and they could not hear any movement from the robbers.

Dieter and Owen's eyes met. They were both thinking about the same act: snatching the watchman's Colt, and shooting their way out of the camp. They would be taking a dangerous chance. Possibly, there was another guard outside of their vision. There could be Blood

Masks awake in the camp. Even if they stole the weapon without startling the lookout, they would have but one revolver against a dozen madmen.

The mortal alternative, though, was to submit to Karl's plans, whatever they may be. Owen knew from the day that Dieter saved his life that the lawman was fearless. Dieter did not need a gentle nudge.

He rose to his feet, and gestured to Owen and Renard to do the same. They froze nervously as Dieter strode over to the sleepy sentinel. The guard was still sat on the rock, his head slumped over, snoring quietly. Dieter was no pickpocket, but the lookout did not awaken when the lawman reached into his holster and snatched the revolver.

Dieter could now see the camp. The Blood Masks were still sleeping contentedly, curled up under their blankets around a now cold campfire. Dieter was most certainly not going to be complacent under the perilous circumstances, yet he was shocked by the Blood Masks' neglect. He noted that even Karl was asleep. The outlaw gang clearly liked to think of themselves as living legends. Having met a few of them, though, he could see that they were hardly the elite of the criminal under-world. Escaping seemed to be a little too easy, so Dieter kept his guard up.

With a wave of his hand, Dieter beckoned Owen and Renard to join him. This time, there would be no tiptoe-ing nor sneaking. Weary as they were, they sprinted back to their horses, which were still tied up at the slope leading to the plateau.

The pummelling of their leather boots on the rocky ground startled the Blood Masks. They looked almost comical as they scrambled out of their makeshift beds. Some attempted to put their shoes on for the chase. Others reached directly for their rifles or revolvers. One of them was particularly rapid, and raised his hand to fire his revolver. Dieter, though, was as perceptive and ruthless as a bald eagle. Without slowing, he turned and fired a bullet into the aggressor. Owen noted that it was the short, fat crook from last night. He was once again smiling childishly as Dieter's round caught him in his clammy forehead. The robber's infantile grin did not fade as he collapsed into oblivion.

In a matter of seconds, that felt like hours to the fleeing men, the camp was a swarm of flying bullets. The wreak of cordite was so heavy that Owen could feel it in his gorge. The terrifying report of the bullets only hastened their strides. It was miraculous that they reached their horses. Renard had to share Owen's roan, and Dieter spurred his horse violently to lead them away.

Calmly lying in his bed, Karl had not slept well. Hearing Renard's lies had bothered him, and he had dwelt on the old man's words before finally sleeping dreamlessly. Being awakened by gunfire had not improved his mood, but he was nevertheless reserved. Karl did not reach for his revolver and give chase because his chess pieces had already been put in place. He knew that the escapees would not get far.

Still panicked, the lawmen rode their horses furiously. They clung to the reins tightly as they ferociously rocked on their mounts, Renard desperately clinging to Owen's back. Owen followed Dieter, and prayed that he knew where he was riding. It was Renard, though, who called for the men to slow. They had been riding for some time, when Renard cried, 'Whoah! Let's stop a moment.'

Breathlessly, Owen and Dieter pulled on their reins. They stopped on a rocky path, where in the early light they had a spectacular view over the desert below them. Chastity and Prospect, as well as other townships further afield, were in plain sight.

'My boys, we're a good few miles away. We cannot maintain this pace all the way home, not on this stony ground. Let's take a moment to think.'

They did. Owen and Dieter did not speak. They only wheezed tiredly, lacking the energy to think lucidly. The three were out of earshot of the bullets, and they could not hear any man nor animal giving chase.

'I cannot hear them setting off after us, boys. Why do you think that is?' Still mounted behind Owen, Renard patted Owen's shoulder as if he were encouraging a schoolboy stuck on a knotty maths problem.

'I don't know, Renard,' was Owen's panted response. 'But let's not wait too long.'

Renard's demeanour changed balefully. 'No. Let's not.'

As alert as Dieter normally was, even in a state of fatigue, even he was taken aback when Renard somehow conjured a revolver and fired into his chest. The force of the gunshot knocked Dieter off his mount, and he fell to the ground dead. The brave man's life had been ended in one single and absurd moment.

The gunshot singing in Owen's ears, he was stunned by the incongruity of the situation. He wondered for a second if he had truly just witnessed his friend Renard murder Dieter.

Renard laughed cruelly, an inhuman bellow that

Owen scarcely recognized. Owen felt Renard's revolver poking into his back.

'Turn around and go back to the camp, Sheriff Rowlands. Take your time. On the way, I will share with you some fascinating revelations.'

CHAPTER 25

Though Owen had his back to Renard during the return to the camp, he did not doubt that Renard was foaming at the mouth. He could feel specks of saliva on his nape as Renard ranted like a madman. Owen was reminded of the town drunk Joshua, except that Renard was no harmless eccentric. The sheriff wondered if the monster sharing his mount was in fact the same person he had shared countless merry nights with.

Owen also thought back to the mysterious day when he had discovered Renard drunk. His intoxicated discourse on Zeus had seemed incongruous. Now, that inexplicable episode appeared oddly telling.

The lawman also felt physically sick. As frightened as he was, the illness in his gut came from witnessing something that simply should not be. He was riding like an automaton, unable to concentrate his mind on the direction of the roan. Though he could hear Renard's ravings, Owen was not following the thread of the old man's exclamations. He mentioned Greek myths, Roman soldiers and European philosophers. Renard repeatedly referred to 'superiority' and 'strength', rhetorically asking Owen whether he agreed.

As they pulled into the camp, Owen expected some manner of sarcastic applause or jeering. However, there was only a reverential silence. The Blood Masks' base appeared to be at work, and the men had busied themselves with clearing the campfire and cleaning their weapons. It struck Owen that the outlaws feared Renard.

'Stop,' Renard commanded. Owen nervously complied. The old man dismounted nimbly, keeping his revolver trained on Owen. 'Now get down from the horse and kneel before me.'

Owen obeyed, falling to his knees in a cruel mockery of a supplication to a king. He looked Renard in the eye, and felt as though Renard did not appreciate meeting him eye to eye.

'As a boy, Sheriff Rowlands, I knew I was different, better. I was both more intelligent and physically stronger. In the classroom and the sports pitch, I bested all. I was not so naïve to think that my great wealth made me superior. I had an inner compulsion, a raging desire to excel, to succeed. To conquer.'

Karl strode over to the two, and stood by Renard's side. He had listened to this story from Renard many, many times. Karl was tired of hearing it.

'When I gave some wretch a hiding in a barroom, or when I put a son in some harlot, I learned that the rules did not control me. I had the intellect and the passion to rise above ordinary men, my lessers. I heard you paid my Aunty Jasmine a social call, huh?'

Owen said nothing.

'I will wager she said something like I ran away in disgrace. Not true, old boy. I did indeed father several sons out of what conventional humans call wedlock. Yet I did not abandon them, my own kinsmen. Indeed, I needed young men who shared my superior blood. My sons are in position all over America. My spawn is everywhere. The Blood Masks – almost all of them are my own descendants. They are a unique tribe of superior men.'

The sheriff could scarcely believe what Renard was proclaiming. His dear friend, with whom he had sipped whiskey and discussed poetry, was also the leader of a brood of killers.

Karl, however, knew all too well the truth of his father's claim.

'When the door to my house closed and you left me alone, you knew not what I was planning. I was no traditional daddy to my killer kindred. I paid their mothers to maintain them, and I looked in on them whenever I could. When they were men, I tore them from their mothers' breasts and brought them here. I have spies all over this land.'

Renard licked his lips maniacally, and continued. 'There were daughters, too – or so I'm told. I have no use for them. Of course, I pay their mothers a pittance to keep quiet. But I want soldiers, fighting men!'

Owen thought of Renard's occasional absences, when he apparently travelled back East. He was sometimes away from Prospect for weeks at a time. Curious, Owen prodded for more information.

'Who was the young man at your house?'

Renard laughed harshly. 'Young Arthur – who in fact has the same mother as Karl, here. Now Karl is one of the finest minds in the state. Arthur, though – well, he did not inherit his brains from his father. He was wild and

127

crazy. My boys informed me that he had run off one night, and the next thing I know he shows up at my house. He was ranting and raving about his work at the gold mine, and how he was going to hold the place up. I was furious, and I struck the stupid boy. We fought, and the brawl was so ferocious that my whole house was wrecked. I finally settled the score. Arthur was no more.'

That's not quite what you told me, thought Karl. Indeed, Karl was growing weary of his father's constant deceptions.

'I had to adapt my plans. The house, my old life in Prospect – no matter. It was all to be abandoned eventually, in any case. I also had to send Karl to deal with you and Jasmine. Sheriff Rowlands, I must admit that you have impressed me with your courage and tenacity. In other circumstances, you would have been an excellent Blood Mask. It is unfortunate that I will have to eliminate you.'

'So what was that business in the cave, last night? Why didn't you just shoot me yesterday?'

'Mere mind games, Sheriff. It amused me to play you along a little further.'

Karl had wondered the same thing. As a boy, Karl had idolized his father and longed to fight by his side in the crusade he would lead. While Karl's loyalty had never swayed, he had begun to wonder if Renard was in fact a sane man. Karl was also appalled by his brother Arthur's fate.

Owen had nothing more to say, nor ask. He naturally had a thousand questions, but felt that he had heard enough. He had to keep Renard, talking, though. The progenitor of the Red Masks obviously adored boasting of his supremacy. This would buy Owen a few valuable moments of living.

Renard cocked his revolver.

CHAPTER 26

Karl had a very healthy opinion of himself and his abilities, an arrogance that his father had drilled into him. Witnessing his father take charge, and hearing his lies, made Karl feel oddly like a little boy, though.

Renard had been absent from the lives of Karl and his brother Arthur for many years. Karl had seen Renard murder and punish other members of the Blood Masks. He had had to purge various errant members himself at certain times. Though the outlaws were – according to Renard – his half-brothers, killing them had never pressed upon his conscience. Arthur was different, though. Perhaps because they had the same mother, and had been raised together, Karl felt more than mere criminal loyalty to Arthur. He felt true brotherly love, though he would never admit this to himself.

Renard was about to murder once again, and the image of his father with his revolver to Owen's head vividly reminded him of a rite of passage from his boyhood.

At school, Karl and Arthur had not mixed well with

the other children. This was partly because they were stigmatized for being fatherless, but mostly because they were trouble. Karl had been devious and sneaky, tricking his classmates into his own greedy schemes. Arthur was hot-headed and wont to give in to his slightest impulses. The teachers and other schoolchildren were always relieved when the boys played truant, which they frequently did.

From their classmates, Karl and Arthur had learned that all the boys had been taken hunting by their fathers, and been blooded. Before Renard's abrupt return into their lives, Karl and Arthur never imagined that they, too, would have this opportunity. They too would be blooded, though, in a hunt for human prey.

That deadly day, Karl and Arthur had abandoned their mother in the fields. She had struggled to discipline them, yet was determined to toil to raise the boys as best she could. Only later did Karl learn that Renard had secretly paid Louanne a pittance towards their upkeep.

They ran off to play in the woods, when they were approached by a strange man. He had a rifle with him and two revolvers. It did not take a great deal of persuading to spirit away two young boys, especially when the stranger professed to be their own father.

Renard had indeed been kind and fatherly to them that day. He had taught them to shoot, heartening their efforts with gentle encouragements. At the time, Karl and Arthur knew very little of their father. Renard, though, seemed to know a lot about them. This was the boys' first encounter with Renard, and certain things he said had a chilling quality about them in retrospect.

'Come on, Karl. You're better than that.'

'Good shot, Arthur. You'll put the fear of God into people.'

Renard had repeatedly emphasized how much better and superior the boys were to others. This was, of course, everything a young child with no father to guide them was desperate to hear.

Their father had led them to another farm, some distance from their mother's. The farm was inhabited by an old bachelor named Tom. Tom was something of a recluse, and a hard drinker. Renard had stressed how Tom was no good, a drunk, a layabout. Their father had described their murder of Tom as a harmless prank. He had winked at the boys, telling them not to tell their mother what they were up to.

When night had fallen, the three had broken down Tom's front door. While he was puffing on his pipe in his chair, the three had opened fire. Renard had fired the first shot, but his boys had copied him enthusiastically. After Tom collapsed to the floor, his body bloodied and sooty from his ordeal, Renard had walked over to the dead man. He had dirtied his finger with Tom's blood, and blooded both his boys on their cheeks.

That was over ten years ago, and at the time it had seemed like an exciting game. Renard had disappeared again, leaving the boys in the care of their increasingly desperate mother. He reappeared from time to time, always with some wicked act to tempt his sons. As an adult, Karl realized that many of the other Blood Masks would have had similar experiences. He had learned that his father had been prolifically promiscuous, and so bent on raising his army that it bordered on insanity.

As a man, he could see that his experiences were

nothing special. At times, he even felt pangs of guilt for the innocents he had murdered, for the trouble he had caused his own mother, and for Arthur. As children, Karl had thought that Arthur was merely a handful, a naughty boy. Growing into manhood with him, Karl had realized that Arthur was not well-equipped for life as an outlaw. He was like an overgrown child, still exhibiting boyish enthusiasms and fantasies. Arthur was also unlike Karl in that Arthur was in fact friendly and gentle. Despite the grave crimes that Renard had led him in to, Arthur had a kind soul.

Renard had glossed over how he had gotten rid of Arthur. Karl had tried to pay it no mind. He was, after all, a de facto prince of the Blood Masks. While he was otherwise a reptilian predator, he felt an unfamiliar sensation when dwelling on the fate of his brother. Shame. Karl's mind played over and over images of Renard cruelly giving Arthur a thrashing. Arthur was a harmless lost soul who, mercurial as he was, had always been faithful to his brothers and his father.

Seeing Renard on the brink of his next murder, Karl felt utterly lonely and pathetic. He wanted to scrub his skin with a wire brush, in arctic cold waters. He had ruined countless lives, and his reward was a barren lair in the hills and the loss of his dear brother.

He drew his revolver and pointed it at Renard.

'Father – no!'

CHAPTER 27

Renard was plainly enraged by Karl's challenge. He turned his weapon from Owen to his son.

'Do you dare to undermine me, boy?! I am your master and your father.'

'Father, this is just getting dumb. We can't kill two sheriffs!'

'I am the Lord of the Blood Masks, boy, and nothing will prevent my conquest!'

'Your "conquest"?' Karl screamed.

This was the first occasion when Owen had seen Karl lose his reserve. Something had troubled him greatly. Perhaps it was Renard's crazed words.

'The Lord of the Blood Masks?! Who the heck do you think you are?'

Renard's absurd boasts filled Karl with pure contempt. His father had conceived of a legion of his sons, growing wealthy through bold raids and daring – yet sophisticated – ploys. Karl knew that the Blood Masks had had their successes from time to time, but he was starting to see them as a ridiculous joke. His father had been born a rich man, and the Blood Masks were his insane fantasy.

'I am your master,' hissed Renard, 'and you will respect me as such. Now put your weapon away or I will extinguish you as I extinguished your idiot brother!'

Owen reflected that he did not know who Renard really was. His old friend – if he could ever have been described as such – was possessed of a self-importance of such magnitude that it had become madness. Owen could see why Karl was pushed to act as he did.

His father's insult to Karl's dead brother – who was also Renard's own son – gave Karl all the rationalization he needed. Through his invented life as Prospect's kind, retired schoolteacher, Renard had hidden his brutal strength and skill with a firearm. Renard was in fact a skilled marksman, but he had trained his son too well.

Karl did not feel as though he had been provoked. Shooting Renard was not a flash of uncontrolled rage. Karl felt as if he was stamping on an insect, or drowning a sick old dog that was no good anymore.

Karl pulled his trigger before Renard had the chance to react. He accurately targeted his shot at Renard's forehead. A bloody mass of flesh and bone was struck from Renard's skull.

Karl strode over to take a look at the fallen emperor. His face was still contorted from his insane rant. Eyes as wild and staring as a gargoyle's, Renard had a truly devilish aspect as he gazed up to the heavens.

The Blood Masks stared at the gruesome tableau in stunned silence. Karl knew they may react, but he was not afraid. This demented adventure had to come to an end, and he was willing to face the consequences.

'The king is dead,' he joked. 'Long live the king.'

Though the Blood Masks were his apparent half-brothers, he felt no great love for them. Despite their father's obsession with the superiority of his bloodline, most of them were idiots and weaklings. Without Renard ordering them around, they would have drifted towards some other bully. His father had often boasted that the Blood Masks were hidden all over America. However, Karl had met few others outside of their desolate bolt-hole in the hills. Perhaps this was part of Renard's whimsy. Who knew?

'OK then, Blood Masks. There's no more Renard to push you around. Anyone want to make a move on me? Make a move. But I'm sick of this stupid life and I had a bellyful of that crazy old man. He was gonna get us all killed. You do what you want, Blood Masks. I'm getting out of here.'

Karl spied one of the brood reaching for his revolver, but once again Karl was too fast. He shot the would-be attacker in the chest, causing him to hurl backwards, skin, blood and bone exploding in ribbons from his breast. As the remaining Blood Masks smelled the cordite and rusty whiff of blood in the air, they decided that Karl had won his argument.

'Sheriff Rowlands,' barked Karl. Owen looked at Karl, but did not speak. 'Get the heck out of here. Get back on your horse and ride before these jerks change their mind. Or I do!'

Owen felt hope that this nightmare would soon be over. He calmly rose to his feet, and took Renard's six-shooter from his lifeless fingers. Owen still felt no warmth towards Karl, who had deceived him and Dieter several times, and had even tried to kill him. He was seeing the assassin in a new light now, though. Owen would never fathom what madcap goings on had occurred behind the scenery of Renard's stage play of a life. He would never know what it was like to grow up under Renard's guiding hand.

The sheriff backed away towards his roan. He had the feeling that he was going to escape alive and intact. The Blood Masks watched him inching away, yet none of them attacked. He could see that their fate had flipped. There were no jeers this time. Without Renard and Karl, the Blood Masks were a directionless rabble. To Owen, backing away slowly, they looked like lost little boys. He felt no pity for them, though.

When he reached his horse, he turned and rode away.

Karl was in the process of doing the same. He gathered a couple of things, and made towards his own horse. Taking action was a pleasing distraction from the emptiness he felt in his soul.

'Boss Man,' cried out one of the outlaws. 'What do we do now?'

'Partner,' Karl replied, 'you are free to do whatever you choose. If you want to stay here and carry on Renard's little tradition, don't let me stop you. Or you could do what I'm gonna do.'

'What's that, Boss Man?'

'I'm gonna find a job. I'm done with the Blood Masks bull.'

CHAPTER 28

The adventure – if it could be described as such – had reached its climax. On his return to Prospect, Owen set his mind to the ugly clearing up that would be needed following the Blood Masks' path of destruction. Jeremiah and Elijah had urged Owen to rest, and he intended to. Firstly, though, there was only one task on his mind. He would lead his men to recover the remains of his lost companion.

Exhausted by his ordeals, Owen felt like a fish swimming in circles when he returned to the base of the Blood Masks. He made sure that he and his deputies were well-armed, but he was certain that he would find the camp abandoned.

He was right. Save for the bodies of Dieter and Renard, the Blood Masks had run away.

So much for your army of superior men, thought Owen.

It was painful to face up to the remains of Dieter, but Owen steeled himself. He would never abandon his friend to the coyotes and the flies. Owen was not able to save his friend, but he would make certain that Dieter's body would be treated with decency and dignity.

He knew so little of Dieter, but the man had lain down his life for Owen. In contrast, Renard – who Owen thought of as a close friend – had attempted to murder him.

How well does anyone know anyone, Owen wondered.

The three lawmen tossed Renard's cadaver, still staring like a gargoyle, over the rocks at the edge of the plateau. The vultures could have him.

Dieter's burial was a very simple affair. The ceremony was not ostentatious, as befitted his stoic nature.

Dieter's family were German by birth, yet they all spoke English strongly. Owen learned that Dieter's parents were still living. He could not estimate their age, but they clearly shared Dieter's reserve and lean features.

The sheriff also had several brothers and sisters. Owen found that he was surprised by this, as Dieter had always seemed to be so solitary. He wondered what kind of upbringing the lawman had enjoyed. Despite all of the hardships they had shared, Owen regretted that he knew very little about his taciturn comrade.

Owen did not doubt that Dieter's relatives were shattered by their loss. However, they hid their grief behind faces as grey and unspeaking as tombstones. Owen was touched by the friendship and welcome that the Hanovers showed him. To his astonishment, Owen learned that Dieter had often spoken very fondly of him to his relatives.

The sun was especially cruel that day. Some of the mourners, clad in funeral black, clearly suffered in the heat. Owen scarcely noticed, though. At the graveside,

Owen clutched Mary's hand so tightly that he feared he would break her fingers. It would be unbecoming of a sheriff to howl with tears, though that was how Owen felt. He had lost a dear and true friend. Dieter had bravely fought at Owen's side several times, and had even prevented his murder. Moreover, Owen's brother in arms acted out of pure dedication and courage. Dieter was driven by his sense of duty, and devotion to the town of Chastity. He had sacrificed himself willingly and in the process helped to rid an evil menace.

After the internment, the funeral party had returned to Dieter's parents' home. The Hanovers had striven in their fields to provide their children with a promising future. Their hopes for their son, though, had been destroyed. While the Hanovers were most hospitable, Owen and Mary felt that they ought not stay long. Though it pained Owen to leave, it was time to leave the Hanovers to their grief.

Leaving Chastity, there was no shortage of well-wishers seeking to shake Owen's hand and thank him for his gallantry. Mary batted them off politely. Owen repelled them impolitely.

There was much less reserve at another ceremony of remembrance, at an anonymous grave in Prospect later that evening. The Blood Masks and their provenance were no longer a secret. Louanne cared not who heard her wails of desolation.

She had not seen Arthur and Karl for a long, long time. She was an old woman now, and too weak to tend to her fields. She had still been receiving a trifling income from Renard. Louanne had long despised her

140

old lover, yet depended on him for her spartan sustenance. When she saw Karl riding up, she knew in her breast that it was to deliver unhappy news. It was telling that he had arrived alone, and his brother Arthur was absent. Since they were boys, whenever the boys came home from wherever they had disappeared to, it portended trouble. For all their crimes and wrongs, her boys stuck together.

Arthur's death was like a physical pain to Louanne. Karl was careful not to share all of the facts of his demise. His mother knew – or had at least guessed – what their father had recruited them into. Indeed, it was Renard's cocksure arrogance and hollow promises that had attracted her to him. She rued the hush money she had accepted from him.

Louanne drew comfort from one thing. Karl had changed. There was an almost imperceptible difference in his normally vain demeanour – but, of course, a mother could tell. Karl, the apparent master criminal, was clearly fighting back tears when he related his account of Arthur's fate. After a little while, Karl stopped fighting and wept into his mother's lap.

At the graveside, Karl consoled his mother with his embrace. He put his arm around her shoulders and drew her near. The sun was setting and the air was cooling. They had always been pariahs, mused Karl. There was no preacher, and no church service. They were the only mourners. Not so long ago, Karl delivered commands to his henchmen from a hiding place in the shadows. Tonight, like his mother, he did not care who knew who he was. Karl was not going to hide anymore.

He gave his mother a squeeze, and she took his hand in hers.

Her boy had come home.

CHAPTER 29

'Good morning to you, Lee. How are you keeping?'

Lee the bartender was pleasantly taken aback when Brother Joshua strolled in that morning.

Despite his drunkenness, Joshua never patronized the saloon. He was cautious of scaring the other customers, and was also aware that intoxicated miners may not be indulgent of Joshua's ways. The seer had never been physically attacked: Sheriff Rowlands forbade it. While Joshua's thoughts did not follow the patterns of ordinary men, he was nonetheless unwilling to tempt fate.

The unexpected visitor surprised Lee Charles in some other ways, too. Lee was familiar with Joshua's rants. Though the barkeeper was skilled at handling belligerent drunks with diplomacy, he had always kept away from Joshua. Lee could tell that he had much deeper problems than a taste for the bottle. However, today, Joshua looked unusually healthy. Joshua was cheerful and upbeat, yet seemed sheepish about something.

'I'm very well, Joshua. How can I help you?'

Lee had always been quietly impressed by Joshua's insane soliloquies. Even when he was fuelled by cheap booze, Joshua could speak eloquently and passionately. From his pulpit in the gutter, Brother Joshua could make almost poetic speeches. Today, though, Joshua was staring at his shuffling feet, and seemed tongue-tied.

Joshua had indeed undergone something of a catharsis. After seeing off Sheriff Rowlands, his mind had been plunged into the blackest nightmares he had yet known. The choirs of tormenting voices had goaded him and chided him. The voices of the angels were angry that Joshua had allowed Owen to endanger himself; the devils boasted that now he was in their clutches. So unrelenting and agonizing were the voices that Joshua had pressed his hands to his ears. There was no respite, and Joshua sank to his knees in unspeakable pain.

He did not know how long he remained that way. It could have been hours and hours, but Joshua had no idea. Just as the choir of angels blocked out all other sound, his visions were all he could see. The images were horrific. Joshua again saw Owen hunted by the monstrous hounds, but this time they gained on him. With hideous yellow fangs, the black wolves bit into Owen. He thrashed for survival, but was blinded by the bloody red mist that cloaked the hell-hounds.

In the dreams – though to Joshua, they were more vivid and painful than what ordinary men call reality – Owen fought on. Joshua knew not how Owen could endure the tearing claws of the ethereal beasts, yet persist Owen did. Within the blackness, Owen's image had begun to glow with all the strength and serenity of a silvery moon. His inner fire was chasing away the darkness and the rusty fog. The demon dogs yelped and panicked, suddenly chastened by a being that was both mightier and better than them.

In his own breast, Joshua felt something stir. It was pleasing to see such hopeful prophecies. As the red mists cleared, and Joshua's earthly eyesight returned, he found himself slumped against a wall in an alley. During the vision, he had perspired feverishly. Joshua found that he was literally soaking wet, as if he had immersed himself in a river. Conscious of his religious nickname, Brother Joshua wondered if – on some level – he had been baptized.

It was a rare moment of hiatus from his mental suffering. He may have resembled a pathetic, sweaty derelict to the passers-by, but Joshua felt well. Indeed, he felt healthier than he had in a long, long time. Resting on the ground, it occurred to him that a man needed to be strong in body and mind to fight through his visions. Joshua had yet to learn what had happened to Owen, but Joshua's vision had inspired him. Just as Owen had faced down a gruesome monster, perhaps Joshua had deeper reserves of fortitude.

Knowing not why exactly, Joshua had called on Doctor Crocker. The doctor had been glad to help. Joshua lacked the funds to pay the physician, but Crocker insisted that Joshua could owe him for the course of medicines he prescribed.

Joshua's next stop was Lee's saloon.

'You see, Lee . . . you know, I hate to ask . . . just wondered if you needed any hired help here at the saloon.' Joshua looked up uncertainly. 'No trouble if you don't.'

Lee could not help but grin. In truth, he had no need for any staff. Lee had always preferred to be his own barman. However, the kind grandfather within him could not resist.

'As it happens, I could use a hand. Won't pay much. As a matter of fact, you can start immediately.'

Joshua's mouth dropped open, and he was once again tongue-tied. He mumbled his acceptance, and hurried himself behind the bar.

'You heard about Sheriff Rowlands, Joshua?'

Joshua had not, and Lee was glad to pass on the story. While Joshua was relieved to learn that Owen had survived, he was startled by the similarities between Owen's ordeal and his own fever dream. It made Joshua wonder if his farsightedness was in fact madness, or whether it was an unwanted gift from another plane of existence. This time, though, Joshua decided not to share his insights.

Joshua was far from cured, if his condition ever could be. He would take his medicines, but doubted if they could truly help him. He would also stay away from alcohol. Deep in his psyche, Joshua knew that the angels would only be speechless for a short time. He was only enjoying a respite, but this short break from his visions gave him great clarity. Joshua was thinking of ways he could adapt, methods for carrying on, even with his evil eye. Though he had been nothing but a nuisance to Prospect, he had also seen that there were many kind individuals who would support him.

Joshua's curse was only dormant. For now, that was enough.

CHAPTER 30

Owen's emotions were a whirlpool. He was grateful to Mary for her patience and love. His experiences had been so odd, so unique that he felt that he had no other he could confide in. On their return to Prospect, Owen could not face returning to the boarding house. The drab single man's room would only have disheartened him further. He invited Mary to take in the cooling early evening air.

They set off on a stroll. Owen was glad to leave the town for a short while. There were too many well-wishers ready to shake his hand and thank him. Owen only desired some time with his sweetheart.

The light was greying as they walked in intimate silence. Mary was greatly worried about her suitor, but did not press him. This was Owen's way, and he would speak when he was ready.

'You can play your part just by being there for him,' Ma Bolton had advised. 'He just wants to know you're by his side.'

The rocky hills were a shadowy black against the dimming heavens. Owen had been in so much danger, but now she imagined the mountains as benevolent guardians of an ancient order. The stony custodians were watching over them from their thrones on the horizon.

Owen and Mary did not stray too far from Prospect. They followed a zigzagging route, and Mary could tell that Owen's thoughts were elsewhere. After some time, Owen began to talk hesitantly.

'Honestly, Mary. All the shocks I've been through. It's made me wonder what's real and what isn't.' Mary took his hand in hers. 'I thought I knew Renard. He was my own teacher when I was a boy. He encouraged me and kept an eye on me. We were friends! Well, I thought we were friends. Turns out I knew nothing about him. Nothing whatsoever!'

The exasperation in Owen's voice was clear. 'How well does anyone know anyone, huh? 'Cept Renard was more than just an eccentric bachelor. A whole lot more! When I learned who he was, and what he had been doing, I wasn't sure if it was the same man.'

Mary squeezed Owen's hand.

'And it got me thinking. I asked myself how well anyone knows anyone. But that's just cynical bull. 'Cause I know you, Mary. I love you and I know you have no secrets. You've opened your arms to me, shared your home with me, loved me, cared for me. I know you and your folks are good people. I know because I've seen you all toiling in your fields. Seen it with my own eyes.

'And Dieter. . . .' Owen's voice was nearly breaking. 'Heck, I really didn't know him so well. And he didn't know me. But he gave up his life. He fought to the end because he believed in something. Something honest and decent. If I've learned one thing, Mary, I've learned that there really is some good in this world. I am not going to walk away from this whole affair as a broken man. I want to walk away a better man.'

The iron resolve in Owen's words made Mary smile. They would put their ordeal behind them.

'And it made me think on something else, Mary. You know I love you and I've explained many times why we cannot wed. Not yet. I was concerned about being the man you deserve. You and Ma and Pa are some of the best people I've ever met. You could do better than a broke schoolteacher with his boarding house. Well, that's what I thought.'

Mary's attention spiked. She wondered where this was leading.

'Now I ain't no romantic. So I want to run this by you. I've been thinking – maybe I should give up this foolish pride. Maybe I should give up the boarding house, and come and live with you – if you'll have me. I'll carry on as the schoolmaster, and I can't give up as sheriff. Not now. But I'll pay my keep. And on top of my jobs, I'll work the farm with you and your folks. What do you say, Mary? Do you think Ma and Pa will agree?'

She had long reassured Owen that she was not interested in riches. Owen was wealthy in a different way. His devotion to educating the youngsters of Prospect, and to serving the town as its law enforcer, were priceless attributes. She loved his kindness, decency and determination. True, he was stubborn and ill-tempered, but these were only reflections of his tenacity and passion. His powerful build and dirty blond hair also gave her feelings that were not so Christian.

Mary was, of course, thrilled. She felt like bounding

up and down in joy. They stopped walking and Mary put her arms around him.

'Sheriff Rowlands.' She beamed flirtatiously. 'Why of course you can! You know Ma and Pa love you like their own. They've suggested it many a time. But. . . .'

Owen knew what was coming.

'I know, Mary. We can't have a Sunday School teacher living in sin.' Owen tried to be serious, but felt so joyous that he could not help smiling broadly. 'However, it would be acceptable were we betrothed.'

Mary flung herself around her man. She had come so near to losing him, yet his bravery and dedication had saved him. It was darkening now, but Mary was not afraid. Not just safe in the muscular arms of Owen, those ancient hills were indeed watching over her, she mused.

During the walk back into town, Mary could scarcely contain herself. She was as chatty and restless as an infant girl. There would be so many people to tell, so much to organize.

Mary also knew in her gut that she and Owen had a lifetime of happiness and excitement ahead of them. Her man had the courage and mettle to confront any danger ahead of them, and she would be at his side.

CHAPTER 31

At Saint Jude, several of the men peered over the edge at the desert below. They noticed the cloud of dust moving towards them. The dirt swirled around the rider like a sandy dandelion.

The mine was not unlike a European castle. Its denizens would see an enemy coming long before he would see them. The miners only gathered out of curiosity. The dusty vortex was likely to be a new recruit. Were it any kind of threat, the hardened men of Saint Jude had no fear. The law did not often come interfering around their camp.

Mordecai noticed the inquisitive crowd, and acted swiftly to break it up.

'Someone coming here to see us, Mordecai,' one of Mordecai's men explained.

The leader of Saint Jude did not enjoy raising his voice, and rarely did so. His age had softened his speech somewhat, but the authority within it did not invite arguments. Some of the miners remembered Mordecai when he was much younger. He had been lean and strong, never afraid of a fight. His reputation as a bruiser always went before him. Even now, many years later, Mordecai did not lead from the back. He ground away in the belly of the mine with an astonishing work rate. Mordecai set an envious example for much younger men. He did seem much younger than his years, however old he was.

Nobody really knew how old Mordecai was. At Saint Jude, nobody knew too much about anyone else. The men laboured together side by side for years – even decades – without developing intimacies.

Mordecai was not happy to see his crew larking around. The mining corporation would keep the operation at arm's length as long as they were seeing results. Saint Jude was largely left to regulate its own affairs, and Mordecai was keen to keep it that way. Unnecessary pauses in the production process were not acceptable to him.

'Leave him to me, whoever he is. Now get off your butts and get back to work.' The miners acquiesced without debate.

Mordecai himself looked out over the sands below. The rider had reached the rocky climb to the mine. Mordecai's eyesight was weakening, and the image of the man in black below was blurred. However, Mordecai had an inkling who it might be.

His men travelled back and forth to Prospect to collect supplies, or take leave from the mine for a short time. They had heard the stories, and made the connections between Owen's investigations at the mine and their encounter with Arthur. Being men with histories they would care to forget, the miners were not ordinarily gossips. However, this unexpected excitement created a whirlwind of loosened tongues. While the facts of the Blood Masks affair were well known by now, the truth did not prevent a pattern of ridiculous embellishments to the tale.

Mordecai was exasperated when he heard the chatter. His team deserved some distraction from their hardships, but Mordecai was saddened by the whole affair. Arthur had been a young man. Though he was rash and impulsive, he had time enough to reset the course of his ship. Perhaps Mordecai and his men could have helped with that. The thought of an over-grown child like Arthur amidst the Blood Masks was upsetting to him. The Blood Masks – and their leader, apparently his own father – would have bullied him and manipulated him. The men of Saint Jude were not angels, but they could have accepted Arthur into their brotherhood.

Mordecai had also heard that Arthur had a brother, who had absconded from the outlaw gang. Arthur had often mentioned having many, many brothers (who were hidden all over America) but Mordecai had dismissed such talk as idle fantasy. Of course, he had since learned that Arthur's wild claims possessed a grain of truth. Arthur's brother was out there, somewhere, and here was a stranger approaching the camp.

The visitor's horse galloped rapidly, and Mordecai could clearly hear the click of hoofs on the hard ground. He awaited at the main entrance. Mordecai had seen sons following their fathers (and in certain cases, their grandfathers) to Saint Jude. When Karl reached the top

153

of the slope, Mordecai recognized him. He could see the resemblance to Arthur plainly. Karl was also only a little older. Mordecai also knew better than to ask too much about a man's past.

'Good day, stranger,' Mordecai greeted Karl. 'What brings you to Saint Jude?'

Karl dismounted. He knew that the miners had known his brother, but wanted to remain silent as to his relationship to Arthur. Karl wanted to start writing a new chapter in his life. Saint Jude was reasonably near to his mother's farm; he would be able to continue his visits. He sought some honest work, but was also happy to remain safely away from any prying policemen. Saint Jude seemed like the right place to start.

'Suh, I'm looking for some work. Never worked down a mine, before, but I ain't afraid of getting my hands dirty. They say Saint Jude's will give anyone a chance. Name's Karl.'

They shook hands and Mordecai smiled. He had encountered individuals from the spectrum of manhood during his career at Saint Jude. Mordecai had refined an accurate judgment of human character.

There was definitely something dubious about Karl, but he also came across as earnest. The black attire and moustache gave him the appearance of a penny dreadful villain, and he had more than a hint of arrogance. A few shifts in the furnace with men who had no indulgence for pomposity would soon knock that vanity out of him.

Mordecai was unable to save Arthur, but perhaps he could do something for this character.

'Karl, what kind of skills and training do you have? You don't know anything about dynamite, by any chance?'

154

Karl's eyes brightened at the mention of explosives. He and Arthur had had much experience with the stuff.

'Dynamite? Funny you should mention dynamite. . . .'

EPILOGUE

The stage coach was well-guarded. It was carrying a chest of gold to be delivered to a bank in San Antonio. The gold was owned by a wealthy rancher, and the owner was not taking any risks. At least, he did not think he was.

Paul and his crew spied the stage from an overlooking hill on the plains. His eyesight was extraordinary. To his men, the coach and its guards only looked like tiny black ants. Paul's vision had been trained by a lifetime on the plains, and a stint as a scout in the Army. He could watch the party with clarity, discerning every detail of his quarry. Paul was assisted by the weather. It was the afternoon, and the divinely blue sky was cloudless. He wondered if the coach party were enjoying the sun, glad of such a clear day.

There were two guards on horseback, and they rode slightly ahead of the stage. Another two men were sat atop the platform of the coach, one at the reins and the other shotgun. Paul's informers told him that there were another two inside the vehicle – armed, of course. There were six men in total. Paul had ten beneath him.

Only six men seemed to Paul to be rather thin. He

156

had received intelligence that the guards were them-selves ex-Army, highly trained and highly experienced mercenaries. Paul had scoffed when he heard this detail. While Paul was never complacent, he had utter confi-dence in his own abilities as well as those of his own troops. The wealthy – and obviously naïve – rancher was probably afraid of Indian raids, or opportunistic brig-ands. The businessman thought he had kept the transfer secret, not even informing the sheriff. He had never con-sidered that a mastermind like Paul would monitor him from afar, learning every detail of his organization, before launching a single, devastating strike.

The only sounds were the distant, almost inaudible, singing of birds and the repetitive clicking of the hoofs of the coach party. Afar, Paul and his men rested in studied silence. His team were outstanding riflemen, but the coach party was too far away. Their approach would alert their prey.

Paul himself watched and waited patiently. He could feel the frissons of excitement running through his men, who were eager to attack, but Paul himself dominated his own passions. The imminent strike, long planned as it was, was merely business.

Paul recalled an occasion many years ago when he had been challenged to a gunfight. He had always regarded such quick-draw contests as infantile, and beneath him. On that day, though, there was no avoiding the problem. Paul's opponent had made the deadly appointment for midday exactly. Shortly before noon, Paul had sat down for a glass of ale in the saloon. It had only taken a few minutes to step outside, ruthlessly shoot his hopelessly mismatched challenger, and return inside to finish his beer. Though Paul found it rather tiresome, the gun-slinger who returned to his glass of ale had been the talk of the town. Nobody braved Paul afterwards.

Paul would attack the coach party with the same cold-bloodedness. He knew that the looming slaughter would cause his heartbeat to quicken, but afterwards, when the gold was his, it would be home to bed. Tomorrow, he would start planning his next operation.

Paul set his mind to listening to the clip of the horses and the groan of the rocking stage coach. His men could scarcely contain their enthusiasm. When Paul judged that the stage was close enough, he spurred his steed. The eleven raiders charged towards the coach party. Now, there was no disguising the report of the hoofbeats. The guards would not stop to wait and see who the approaching men were. They would open fire instinc-tively. Paul did not intend to allow them the opportunity.

Expertly, Paul could ride at great pace while operating a rifle. He fired his weapon at the first guard, cruelly landing a bullet in his face. The mercenary fell from his horse, hopelessly clawing at the bloody mess.

Contemporaneously, one of Paul's marksmen deliv-ered the same treatment to the second guard on horseback.

The driver of the coach desperately yanked on the reins while the shotgun rider attempted to shoot the raiders. Paul and his men were too fast and too well-orga-nized. Paul had drilled his men to spread out across the plain, such that the coach guards could not get a clear shot. The marauders positioned themselves so that the guards inside the coach could not see them clearly. Within seconds, the attackers rained down a hail of bullets. The shots splintered the wood of the stagecoach, and there was no escape for the mercenaries. Their bodies were riddled by dozens of agonizing wounds.

Two of Paul's men entered the coach, and unloaded the gold into sacks. The weight of the precious metal meant that they had to share the load amongst the whole crew. Paul could see that his informers had been accurate: he had seized a valuable prize. The gold carefully packed onto the horses of the raiders, they set off.

Paul had heard what happened to his brothers in Prospect. He was disappointed, but not surprised nor saddened. That particular division of the Blood Masks had indeed been a rabble. Though Renard had been both his leader and his father, Paul barely knew the man. Paul had also noted that in recent years, Renard had grown particularly crazed. He had wondered how long it would be before Renard made a fatal error. There was no sign of Karl, and Paul wondered if he, too, had been killed.

It seemed to Paul that he was the natural successor to the leadership. He had long commanded his own troop of Blood Masks, and there were no other pretenders to the control. Paul had great ambitions for himself and his men. The rumours described them as thieves and outlaws, but Paul (inspired by his father) saw the Blood Masks as much more than ordinary criminals.

The loss of the Prospect crew was but a scratch from a needle. The Blood Masks were everywhere.